*About the Author*

Gordon Snell is a well-known scriptwriter and author of books for children and adults. Among his books are *Cruncher Sparrow High Flier, Cruncher Sparrow's Flying School, Dangerous Treasure* and *The Mystery of Monk Island*. He divides his time between Dublin and London.

# THE TEX & SHEELAGH OMNIBUS

## GORDON SNELL

*Children's*
POOLBEG

Published 1996
by Poolbeg Press Ltd
123 Baldoyle Industrial Estate
Dublin 13, Ireland

Tex & Sheelagh 1992
The Joke Thief 1993

A catalogue record for this book is available from the British Library.

ISBN 1 85371 631 6

Illustrations by Mary Murphy
Cover design by Poolbeg Group Services Ltd
Set by Poolbeg Group Services Ltd in Stone 12/17
Printed by The Guernsey Press Ltd,
Vale, Guernsey, Channel Islands.

*For dearest Maeve, with all my love*

# Contents

# TEX & SHEELAGH

# 1

## Cat Shelter

"I wonder what kind of homes they'll find for us," said Tex.

"Why can't we stay here?" asked Sheelagh.

"This is only a Shelter, it's where they keep kittens till they find somewhere they can stay for good."

"What happens in a home?" Sheelagh asked. Like Tex, she was about three months old. She had been found by a milkman in an open dustbin. She didn't remember how she got there, so she didn't know what a home was like.

Tex had been born in a good home, but the people were going abroad. So there he was, a ginger kitten with a white chest and shining yellow eyes, waiting and wondering what the future would bring.

"A home is where people live," he told Sheelagh. "Humans, like Mrs Lynch who runs the Shelter here."

"What was *your* home like?"

"It was big. It had lots of different rooms with chairs and tables and beds in them. People seem to need more things than we do. There were machines too, with doors. They put plates in one, and clothes in another, and the machines whooshed and whirred, and the things came out clean."

"Why didn't they put the plates and clothes in the same machine?" Sheelagh asked.

"I don't know. People are odd. You'll find that out, soon enough."

"Catch it, catch it, catch it!" called a big black cat, named Guinness, dashing past Sheelagh and nearly knocking her over. He was chasing a ping-pong ball which he kept hitting ahead of him with his paws. Guinness was black and white, the same colours as Sheelagh, and was always running around chasing things.

Sheelagh joined in, and ran after the ball. So did Tex, and so did an orange-coloured cat called Butterscotch. Soon all four of them were tumbling around, having mock fights with each other. They looked like a bunch of wrestlers.

After a few minutes, the game stopped as suddenly as it had begun. Guinness decided it was time to do a bit of cleaning, and began licking his left leg. Butterscotch lay down and went to sleep.

Tex began helping Sheelagh to stay clean, by licking the back of her neck, under her left ear. They had both discovered that there were bits of their fur it was hard to reach yourself, so they often helped each other like this.

"Thanks, Tex," said Sheelagh. Then a puzzled look came over her face. "What do cats do if they live on their own?" she wondered. "Do the humans help to clean the difficult bits with their tongues?"

"Humans cuddle cats, but they don't lick them," said Guinness, breaking off from his cleaning.

"Maybe they would if we asked them to?" asked Sheelagh.

"I don't think so," said Tex. "Besides, there's no point in asking them things like that. They don't understand what we are saying."

Sheelagh was amazed. "But we understand *them*. At least, I understand Mrs Lynch—and the people who come here to look us over."

Tex said: "They think we only have a few words, like MIAOW and PURR and HISS."

"Yet they often talk to *us*," said Guinness. "It's a mystery."

Tex finished licking under Sheelagh's left ear, and began on the right one.

"It would be awful if they took you and me to separate homes, and we couldn't clean for each other," Sheelagh said.

Tex stopped licking. He looked sad. Then he smiled. He was a cheerful cat, and thought difficulties could always be solved, if you got up and did something about them.

"We'll show them how friendly we are," he said, "then they'll take us both."

"You'll be lucky if they do," said Guinness.

5

He was fond of looking at the gloomy side of life. In fact, in a curious way, saying gloomy things seemed to make him happy.

The cats in the Shelter were kept in a big wooden shed attached to the back of the Lynches' house. It had lino on the floor, and rugs and baskets for the cats to lie on.

That afternoon, they heard Mrs Lynch talking to some people in the house, just outside the door of the Cat Shelter.

"I'm sure you'll see one you like," she said, "and if you do, I can bring it out to your house."

"Can't we take it with us?" asked a woman's voice.

"We always like to bring them to the new home ourselves," said Mrs Lynch, "just to settle them in."

"Good idea," said a man. "Then you can see if *we're* suitable for the cat, as well as the other way round."

"Well, yes—that is sort of the idea," said Mrs Lynch.

She did indeed want to make sure the homes the cats went to were all right. "Anyway," she went on, "come through and have a look at the ones we've got."

The cats looked up curiously as Mrs Lynch brought the two visitors in. There were seven cats in the Shelter. Most of them had been found, like Sheelagh, lost and abandoned.

"We've never had a cat before," said the woman, Moira.

"I was more of a dog person, really," said her husband, Dick.

"Dogs are stupid," said Guinness.

"Oh, listen! he miaowed at us," said Moira.

"You see what I mean?" said Guinness to Tex and Sheelagh. "Humans can't understand us."

Mrs Lynch said: "Cats get very fond of you, just like dogs. But they don't get lonely like dogs do—especially if there are two of them together."

Moira looked at Dick. "What about it? If we're getting one, why not get two?"

Dick said: "They'd be company for each other."

Tex whispered to Sheelagh: "They seem very

nice people—and not bossy."

"Yes, they seem kind," said Sheelagh.

"Let's go for it, shall we?"

"Let's!"

"Okay—act affectionate," said Tex. He began to rub his head against Sheelagh's side, purring loudly.

Sheelagh purred too, and looked up at Dick and Moira with her big green eyes. Then she lay down and rolled over on her back, and put her legs in the air.

"Ah, look at her!" said Moira. "She wants her tummy tickled." She bent down and stroked Sheelagh.

Tex walked across to Dick and stood on his back legs, with his paws on Dick's leg. He gazed up and gave a soft Miaow.

"He's affectionate too," said Dick. He put his fingers down towards Tex, who licked them. Dick laughed. "Just look at him!" he said.

Both the kittens purred even more loudly.

"They're wonderful!" said Moira.

"A pair of beauties!" said Dick. "We'll take them both."

Tex and Sheelagh smiled at each other. They were on their way to a new home.

# 2

# The New Home

That evening, Mrs Lynch and her daughter Deirdre put Tex and Sheelagh into the big cat basket, and placed it on the back seat of the car. As the kittens travelled to their new home, they learned more about Dick and Moira.

"Do you think they'll look after them properly?" Deirdre asked her mother.

"I'm sure they will," said Mrs Lynch, "and they'll be at home more than many people. They're both writers, so they work at home a lot."

"I hope they give them enough to eat," said Deirdre.

"So do I," said Tex.

"Listen to them miaowing in the basket!" Deirdre turned towards the back seat and said:

"It's all right, we're nearly there—it won't be long now."

"Here they are!" said Mrs Lynch, putting the basket down on the living-room carpet, and opening the lid.

Tex and Sheelagh looked out. High above them, they saw the smiling faces of Moira and Dick, gazing down.

"Welcome to your new home!" said Moira.

The two kittens clambered out of the basket and looked around. They were in a big room with a green carpet wall to wall, and large, comfortable-looking armchairs and a sofa, with cushions on it.

"We made them a bed, over here in the corner," said Dick proudly.

"That will be fine," said Mrs Lynch.

Tex and Sheelagh looked across the room. There was a shallow wooden box in the corner, with one side cut away, and a piece of fluffy brown carpet in it.

"And the litter tray's in the other corner," said Moira, pointing to a blue plastic tray full of what looked like stone-coloured gravel.

"Will we need to train them to use it?" Dick asked.

"No," said Mrs Lynch, "cats are such clean creatures. They'll find it for themselves, and know what it's for."

"Of course we will," said Tex to Sheelagh.

"Listen to him miaowing!" said Moira. "Can I pick him up?"

"Of course," said Mrs Lynch.

Moira squatted down and put her hands out. "Come along, Tex," she said, scooping him up. She held him close to her and stroked him. She smelt of some pleasant perfume. Tex began to purr. He felt very comfortable.

Dick picked Sheelagh up and stroked her. His woollen sweater was warm. She looked up at him, and saw him smiling down at her, gazing at her with his big brown eyes. She began to purr too.

"They look as if they're going to be happy here," said Mrs Lynch.

When Mrs Lynch and her daughter had gone, Dick went and got a bowl of food from the kitchen and put it down on the tiled hearth in front of the fireplace. Tex and Sheelagh went across to it. Dick and Moira sat down and watched them eat.

"The people who make these bowls must think cats can actually read," said Moira. "Look, it says CAT on the side of the bowl."

Dick laughed. "Perhaps it's to prevent *us* from eating the cats' food by mistake!"

When they had licked the bowl clean, Tex and Sheelagh did a bit of cleaning of themselves. Then Tex said: "That's what I really like—a nice warm fire!" He got as close as he could to the grate, and sat looking into the flames. "It's kind of them to light it for us," he said.

Sheelagh stretched out on the carpet in front of the fire, and rolled over on her back to warm the white fur of her stomach. She put all four legs in the air.

"Oh, isn't she beautiful?" said Moira, kneeling down beside her and stroking her fur. Sheelagh liked the feeling. She began to purr happily.

Tex's eyes were beginning to close, as the warmth of the fire made him feel sleepy.

Moira picked Sheelagh up and sat down on

the sofa, with the kitten on her lap. Sheelagh felt safe and warm. Her eyelids were getting heavier... and heavier...

A little later, Sheelagh was woken from her doze by the sound of voices in the corner of the room. They weren't the voices of Dick and Moira, who were sitting quietly in their chairs. They came from a big black box that was standing on a small table.

The box was flashing with patterns and colours which changed all the time. Sheelagh thought perhaps there was a fire inside it. She looked at Tex. He was lying down, asleep.

She jumped off Moira's lap and walked warily across to the box and sat in front of it, gazing at the bright changing colours. If there was a fire in there, it certainly didn't give out any heat.

She heard Moira laugh. "Just look at her! She's watching the telly!"

Tex looked up drowsily. He knew about television, from the house he had lived in before. He realised Sheelagh was puzzled and went across and sat beside her.

"What is it?" Sheelagh asked. "If it's another fire, I don't think much of it."

"It's called television," said Tex. "Telly, for short. People spend hours just staring at it."

"Why?"

"I don't know. It's a mystery. Like a lot of things people do."

Tex and Sheelagh wandered back towards the fire. They heard Moira saying their names, and tapping the sofa she was sitting on. Sheelagh went over and jumped up onto it. She purred as Moira stroked her back, then she climbed onto Moira's lap and lay down. Tex walked across to Dick, and jumped onto the arm of his chair. He put his front paws up on Dick's shoulder, and licked his ear. Dick stroked his back. Then Tex curled up too, and closed his eyes, while the television voices droned on.

Before long, Tex began to hear another sound. It was like a kind of human purring. He opened one eye and looked up. Dick's eyes were closed, and his head had sunk forward on his chest. The purring sound was his heavy, steady breathing. Dick was fast asleep.

Moira gave a loud cough. Dick woke up, startled, and said: "Yes? What?"

Moira said: "I think it's time for bed."

"I must have nodded off," Dick said. "I wasn't snoring, was I?"

"Let's just say you were breathing loudly!"

Dick grinned. He got up and began turning off the lights and the gas fire and the television.

"We'll leave one of the lights on," he said. "I know cats are meant to be able to see in the dark, but they probably need a little bit of light to do it."

"How sensible," said Tex to Sheelagh.

"Here's your bed," said Moira, kneeling down beside the box with the bit of carpet in it. Tex went over and sniffed. It smelt dusty. He sat down in front of it.

"I'm sure they'll get into it when we go," said Dick, yawning.

"I'm sure they will," said Moira. "Well, goodnight, cats!"

Tex and Sheelagh both miaowed in a friendly way, as Dick and Moira went out of the door into the hall.

They heard Dick say: "We'll shut them in here for tonight—they've got their bed and litter-tray, and a bowl of water. Tomorrow, we can show them the cat-flap."

They heard another door close, in the distance. Dick and Moira had gone to their own bed. Sheelagh hoped it was more comfortable than the cats' bed seemed. She stood in it and sniffed around. The smell of dust was very strong. She looked at Tex. "I don't think so, do you?" she said.

"No, it's not for us," said Tex. He walked over and sprang onto the sofa. "This will suit me much better."

"And I'll take this one," said Sheelagh, jumping onto one of the armchairs. She stretched happily, then curled up and went to sleep.

# 3

## The Strange Machines

Next morning, Sheelagh woke up early when she heard someone move across the room. She saw Moira go to the window and pull the curtains aside. Daylight filled the room. Tex opened his eyes lazily, then went back to sleep.

"Hello, Sheelagh. Hello, Tex!" said Moira. She tickled Sheelagh behind her ears. "Well, I see you found your own beds!" she smiled. "I'll get you your breakfast, as soon as I've washed and dressed."

She went out of the room. Sheelagh sat up and stretched. She looked around at their new home—at the snug chairs, the fireplace, and the strange television box where the colours and voices had been.

She decided to explore the rest of the house.

She jumped off the chair and went out, the way Moira had gone. There was a big hall with a number of doors leading off it, and a circular wooden staircase at one end. From behind one of the doors, she heard the sound of water gushing. She pushed the door and went in. Then she rushed out again, back to the room where they had slept.

"Tex, Tex! Wake up!" she cried, scratching at the sofa.

Tex sat up, blinking his eyes. "What's the matter?"

"It's Moira!" said Sheelagh in alarm. "She's lost her fur!"

"What do you mean?"

"I followed her, and she's in a place with water pouring down on her, and she's got no fur! She might drown, or die of cold! We must help her!"

Tex laughed. "Don't worry, people do that every day. It's their way of washing. They haven't got any real fur, so to keep warm they have lots of different kinds of fake fur, and they take it off to wash."

"But all that water...!"

"It's a shower. They can't get clean by licking, like we can. In fact, they need help to do a lot of things cats can do without any bother."

"I'm glad I'm a cat, and not a human."

"Oh sure, we're very lucky. And humans respect us. They realise we're cleverer creatures than they are, so they admire us, and give us homes to live in with them, and food to eat."

"That reminds me, I'm hungry!" said Sheelagh.

Just at that moment, they heard Moira calling: "Puss, puss, puss, puss, puss!"

"She means us," said Tex, leaping down off the sofa and rushing towards the sound. Sheelagh followed. They both crashed into Moira's legs as she came out of the kitchen, carrying the bowl with CAT on the side of it. She put the bowl down on a mat, just in front of a glass door that looked out onto a small garden. Sheelagh and Tex began to eat their breakfast.

Afterwards, they started cleaning themselves, and then Sheelagh went off to the litter tray.

When she came back, she found Moira and Dick looking at her in admiration.

"They do know how to use it! Clever Sheelagh!" said Dick.

Sheelagh rubbed against his legs, and he stroked her. Tex decided he deserved a bit of praise too, so he went off to the litter tray and came back to be admired.

Dick and Moira showed them some toys to play with. There was a ball with a bell inside it, and a furry toy mouse. The two kittens dashed around the room chasing them for a while. Then they had a pretend fight, which looked so ferocious that Moira and Dick were afraid they'd hurt each other. But at the end, Tex and Sheelagh sat up and grinned.

"Aren't they just wonderful?" said Moira.

"I could watch them all day," said Dick, "but I suppose we'd better get to work."

They climbed the circular stairs, which had wooden steps that spiralled up to the floor above. The kittens watched them from below.

"I wonder if they'll follow us," said Moira, as they disappeared above. The stairs looked very high, like a steep wooden mountain.

"Come on!" said Tex boldly, "we're going up!"

He climbed onto the first step, then the second. He gave a little jump, and was on the third. He jumped again, and stopped to look back. Sheelagh was still down at the bottom. She drew her breath, and jumped, then jumped again. Soon she was on the step beside Tex.

"It's not as hard as it looks!" she said.

Before long, they were at the top of the stairs. They looked around. They were in a big room, full of light, with windows all along one wall, and glass doors leading out onto a terrace with tubs of flowers on it. In front of the windows there was a long desk taking up the whole length of the wall.

Dick sat at one end of the desk, and Moira at the other.

They were both tapping with their fingers on a board with markings on it, and staring at screens on the desk in front of them.

As they tapped, marks appeared on the screens. Sheelagh was curious to see what they were, so she jumped onto the back of Dick's chair, and then up onto his shoulder to look. Dick gave a cry of surprise, and Sheelagh jumped down onto the desk in front of him.

"Hello, Sheelagh!" said Dick. "Have you come to watch us at work?" He started to stroke the black and white kitten, and Sheelagh purred in a friendly way.

"Come on, Tex," said Moira. Tex jumped onto her lap and gazed at the screen with its strange markings. Then he put his paws up on the keys to get a closer look.

"He's decided to help us write the story!" Moira laughed, as a line of extra marks appeared after Tex had touched the keys. "Mind you, Tex, I don't think a whole line of capital ZEDS is going to mean much to the readers!"

She lifted Tex's paws down from the keys, and stroked him. He purred for a while, then jumped onto the long desk and walked across to where Sheelagh was sitting beside Dick's screen, gazing at it.

"What are they doing?" she asked. "Is this the same kind of screen as the voice-box downstairs?"

25

"It does look like a television," said Tex. "But it only has these marks, which they seem to make themselves, by tapping those keyboards."

Just then Dick tapped another key, and a machine beside the screen began to make a loud, chattering noise. Tex and Sheelagh jumped away, to a safe distance along the desk. A piece of paper with marks on it began to come slowly out of the machine.

"They don't like the noise of the printer," said Dick.

"Never mind, cats, it won't be for long. The page will soon be finished."

Soon the sound stopped, and Dick pulled the paper from the machine and began to look at it.

"Now I know what they're doing!" said Tex. "Dick's reading—that's what they call it. There are words on the paper, which he's put there himself with that machine. They call that writing, and sometimes they do it with a stick called a pen. Remember, Mrs Lynch said they were both Writers."

"But what is it for?" Sheelagh asked.

"It's a way of talking. One person puts words on the paper, and another person reads it."

"Could cats learn to do that?"

"I'm sure we could, if we wanted to. But we don't need to. We are clever enough already."

Sheelagh decided to leave Dick and Moira to their screens, and explore. She wandered round the big room, which was lined with shelves full of books. Tex told her that these were full of writing too.

He curled up on the floor under a table, while Sheelagh went across to the top of the stairs. She looked down. The steps curved down and down below her. They didn't look as easy to get down as to climb up.

She decided to try. She put her front paws out over the edge, then let the rest of her slide off the top step. So far, so good. But there were a lot more steps to go. After she'd gone down six steps, she looked through the open banisters to see how far away the ground was now.

It still looked a long way. She felt dizzy. As she looked over, her paw slipped, and she lost her balance. She gave a little cry, as she began to fall through the empty air.

# 4

## Close Encounters

Though the fall could not have lasted more than a second, Sheelagh felt it was much longer. First there was the feeling of having nothing to hold on to. Her paws flapped at the air as she fell, upside down.

Then she flipped over in the air, and she was on the ground! A shudder went up through her paws and legs, a gasp of air came out of her chest. Then she rolled over on her back and lay there, breathing heavily.

She heard cries from above, and the clatter of feet on the wooden stairs, as Dick and Moira came rushing down, with Tex scampering behind them.

"Are you okay, Sheelagh?" he asked.

"I am, but I feel a bit dazed," said Sheelagh. "I must have slipped. I thought I was going to crash on the floor. Then my paws somehow got themselves stuck out the right way to land."

"We cats know how to fall, we're born knowing," said Tex proudly. He gave Sheelagh a friendly lick behind the ears.

"Look—he's feeling sorry for her," said Moira. She and Dick were shocked at Sheelagh's fall. They stroked her and petted her. To show them she wasn't hurt, Sheelagh got up slowly, stretched, and walked across to the back door, which looked out onto the garden.

"Shall we let them out?" Moira wondered.

"Yes, let's show them the cat-flap we put in the door," said Dick.

"They're standing right beside us. Why can't they just open the door?" asked Tex, who was beside Sheelagh, looking out through the glass of the door at the small, walled garden.

"What is a cat-flap?" said Sheelagh.

31

"It's a special door for us, so that people don't have to come and open the big door when we want to go in and out," said Tex. "People are really very lazy."

"Here's your door, kittens," said Dick, kneeling down and pushing the flap so that it swung to and fro on its hinges.

"I wonder if they understand," said Moira.

"It looks dead simple to *me*," said Sheelagh, and pushed her way through the flap. Tex followed her.

"Clever cats!" they heard Moira cry.

The two kittens looked around. The garden was like a small courtyard, with a paved area in the middle, and flower-beds around the edge. On the paved part there was a round table and two chairs, made of metal and painted white.

There were flowers and bushes in the beds, and leafy plants growing up the high walls around the courtyard. In the back wall there was a gate made of black metal that curled and curved in a pattern. They could see through the gaps in the metal shapes.

Outside, there was a grassy lane, and a wooden fence opposite.

The kittens began to explore the garden, sniffing with pleasure at the flowers and the plants and the earth. For a while Dick and Moira watched them through the glass door. Then Dick said: "I suppose we'd better get back to work."

"Suppose they can't work the flap to get back in again?" Moira was worried.

"Let's show them!" said Sheelagh. The two kittens dashed back through the cat-flap.

"Marvellous!" said Moira. "I must ring up my mother and tell her how clever they are!"

The kittens ran out through the cat-flap again.

They began to explore the small garden, weaving in and out among the flowers and plants, and sniffing at everything.

There were smells everywhere. On the earth they could smell traces of other cats, and of animals strange to Sheelagh.

Tex said he thought he smelt mice, which were fun to chase. He had seen one in the garage of the first home he'd been in, and run round and round after it. But it had been too quick for him, and all that happened was that Tex knocked over an open paint-can that was on a shelf.

The paint spilt, and his tail had a green stripe for a while after that. The car had some splodges of green on it, too. Tex thought they looked nice, but the people in the house didn't seem to agree.

Sheelagh looked round excitedly. Perhaps she would see a mouse here and chase it. But all she saw was a grey tube-like creature, wriggling. She picked it up, but it felt all squishy and slimy and it squirmed in her mouth, so she dropped it again. At once, it burrowed down into the earth, and disappeared.

She padded along, sliding through the narrow space between a big blue-flowered bush and the wall. Something tickled her forehead, and then she found filmy white strands across her eyes and whiskers. As she brushed them away, she saw a small black creature with a lot of legs, scurrying up the wall. She had disturbed a spider's web.

Then, in another smaller bush nearby, she heard a buzzing sound. She went across to it. The buzz was coming from one of the yellow flowers. It stopped. Sheelagh poked her nose towards the flower, and saw inside it a yellow·and black fuzzy ball, with wings on it.

She was just going to sniff at it, when Tex leaped across the garden, stretched out both paws, and pushed her away. She fell down on the earth of the flower-bed. She sat up, blinking, and looked at Tex.

"What did you do that for?" she asked, grumpily.

"You ought to be thanking me," said Tex. "I saved you."

"Saved me?"

"That's right."

As he spoke, the furry ball flew out of the flower and buzzed away into the sky.

"That's a bee!" Tex went on. "They don't just buzz—they sting too! Remember, not all the creatures you find in places like this are friendly."

And indeed, very soon Sheelagh met another creature who was very unfriendly indeed.

# 5

# The Growling Beast

Sheelagh promised Tex she'd be careful. She told him about the other creatures she had met.

Tex nodded. "The wriggly one's a worm," said Tex, "and the other is a spider. They're foolish creatures. One just burrows up and down in the ground all day, and the other one weaves silk webs that get in our way."

"They're not very tasty."

"No, they're useless as food for us. Imagine going out hunting worms! We won't need to do any hunting, anyway. Dick and Moira have decided to be our food providers. Humans like doing things for cats, it's their nature."

"That's lucky for us," said Sheelagh.

"Well, they realise we deserve it, I suppose," said Tex. "Of course, even though we get our meals, it's still fun to chase things. Like that bird, for instance."

He pointed to a sparrow that was hopping about on a bush. Then he called out: "Stay clear! Tex is here!" and launched himself with a great leap at the bush. The branches weren't strong enough to hold him, so he tumbled to the ground, while the bird gave a twitter and flew away to the safety of a tall tree, in the garden on the other side of the lane.

Sheelagh watched it go. "I wish I could do that."

"Fly like a bird?" said Tex, picking himself up.

"Yes. If only cats had wings!"

"If cats had wings," said Tex, "we could rule the world!"

They went across to the gate with the twisty metal pattern, and peered out into the lane. All they could see was some scattered gravel and tufts of grass, and the solid wooden fence beyond.

"Let's try and get out there," said Tex. "I'm sure we can squeeze through one of these gaps in the metal."

He put his head through one of them. It went through easily. Then he began to slide his body through. Sheelagh put her head through another gap. Her body followed easily, and she was outside the gate.

She looked back, to find that Tex was stuck in the gap.

"I'm wider than I thought," he said.

Sheelagh looked at him, and began to laugh.

"It's not funny!" Tex grumbled. "I could be stuck here for ever. I could be stung by bees, or nibbled by mice, or eaten by tigers."

"What are tigers?"

"Never mind what tigers are!" Tex snapped. "Help me get out of here!"

Sheelagh went back to the other side of the gate. She leaned her shoulder against Tex's backside, and pushed. Then she pushed again. With a grunt, Tex fell out through the gap. Sheelagh joined him outside the gate.

"Thanks," said Tex. "Good team-work there!"

He decided to take a walk down the lane. It ran in a curve, with the backs of houses and gardens on each side. As Tex wandered off down the lane, Sheelagh looked at the fence opposite the gate they had come through. It was made of overlapping slats of wood, so there was no way of seeing what was beyond. Sheelagh was curious to find out.

She crept along beside the fence, where clumps of grass and weeds grew. She went slowly, pausing to enjoy the various smells along the way. Soon, she came to a place in the fence where one of the slats of wood had slipped, and there was a small gap. Sheelagh looked through it.

She could see a large area of grass, with flower beds at the edge of it, and a round pond in the middle. Near the fence just beside her there was a tall tree—the one the bird had flown into. At the far side, near the house, there were paving stones, and some white chairs and a table. There was no-one in the garden.

Sheelagh put her left paw into the gap and pushed.

The slat of wood slipped further down, leaving enough room for her to get through.

She sniffed the air. There was the same pleasant mixture of smells in this garden as in Dick and Moira's, but added to them was the smell that came from the newly cut grass.

Sheelagh walked slowly across the grass, sniffing it. Here and there she found traces of another smell, one that she didn't much like. It was a creature of some kind, but she had no idea what it was.

Then, beside the pond, she saw a little brown bird like the one that had been on the wall. It was pecking at the grass. Sheelagh decided to chase it the way Tex had done. She bounded across the lawn, calling out: "Stay clear! Sheelagh's here!"

At once the sparrow flew off, up into the tree, and landed on a little wooden platform with a kind of house on it, which was fixed to the trunk.

Delighted with herself, Sheelagh walked jauntily towards the pond, and sat down at the edge. She gazed into the water. Then she put her head down to look more closely. She blinked in surprise. A shadowy shape that looked like the head of another cat seemed to be lurking in the water.

Were there some cats that lived underwater? She didn't like water herself, and only drank sips of it now and then. She couldn't imagine getting into it, and certainly not living there. She shook her head from side to side. The cat in the water seemed to do the same.

Warily, she put out a paw and touched the surface of the water. It broke up in ripples, and the shape disappeared.

But she saw some other shapes in the pond. They were orange-coloured and wriggled as they moved through the water. Perhaps if she could put her paw in, thought Sheelagh, she could scoop one of them out. She leaned over the edge of the pond, and stretched her left paw—but that was as far as she got in her fishing expedition.

Suddenly, the peaceful air of the garden was shattered by a loud, harsh noise. It was a roar that hit Sheelagh's ears like thunder. It came from round the side of the house, and as Sheelagh looked across, she saw a huge beast rushing towards her.

It was creamy white in colour, and had long legs. Its nose stuck out much more than a cat's, and its open mouth showed sharp teeth and a large, drooling tongue.

What could it be, Sheelagh wondered, as she stood there, frozen with fright. Perhaps it was a tiger! Now she could see why Tex had been so afraid of tigers eating him up.

The beast was bounding across the lawn towards her. He would soon be near enough to grab her in those slobbering jaws. In panic, Sheelagh began to run.

She ran first towards the fence where she had come into the garden, but she couldn't find the gap. She tried scrabbling up the fence, but couldn't get enough of a grip, and fell off.

The beast had nearly reached her. His jaws snapped, but missed, as she darted away, across the grass and in behind some bushes beside the house. She crouched down on the ground, trying to be invisible.

But the growling beast came pounding across after her, crashing his way through the bushes. She darted out again onto the grass, looking round wildly. Where could she go to get out of reach? The big tree was her only hope. She ran across to it, jumped, and managed to cling onto a broken twig that stuck out of the trunk. She dug her claws into the bark, and heaved herself up a little higher. She was able to scramble onto the next branch above.

The beast was at the tree now. He stood up on his back legs and stretched upwards. His nose touched the tip of Sheelagh's tail, which was hanging down from the branch. Sheelagh quickly snatched her tail away.

The beast was growling and snapping. Sheelagh clawed her way up the trunk to the next branch, then the next. Just above her she could see the wooden platform with the little bird-house on it. Easing herself up beside it, she leaped over and landed on the platform.

She lay down on the platform, her small black and white head peering over the edge at the ferocious creature below. She was safe

from him now. But how would she ever get
down again?

# 6

## The New Gang

The creature started to make yapping sounds as it sat there staring at Sheelagh. She thought it was trying to say something, and the message certainly wasn't friendly.

Then she heard the voice of Tex calling: "Sheelagh! Sheelagh! Where are you?"

"I'm here!" Sheelagh called back. "Up here, in the tree!"

She looked down. Tex was in the lane on the other side of the fence.

"Hold on a minute," said Tex, "I'll come up." A little way along the lane there was a dustbin. He jumped onto it, and from there onto the top of the fence. He walked along it till he was beside the tree.

"That beast chased me," Sheelagh said. "I only just got away. Is it a tiger?"

Tex smiled. "No, it's only a dog. Did you never see a dog before?"

"I don't remember. Not like that one, anyway. He's very fierce. He was going to eat me."

"Dogs aren't as fierce as they pretend. I've heard people say that their bark is worse than their bite."

"What is the dog saying?"

"I can't quite make out," said Tex. "Dogs have funny accents." He looked straight at the dog and said: "Here, you! Can't you talk a bit more slowly?"

The dog stared at Tex. "Who are *you*?" he asked, slowly enough for the kittens to understand.

"We're Tex and Sheelagh," said Tex. "We've just moved in to the house across the lane."

"Well, I live *here*," said the dog, "and I look after the Rooney family in that house. No-one is allowed into my garden without my permission."

"Well, how could you expect Sheelagh to

know that? You're just a bully, that's what you are."

"No, I'm not. Guard dogs are supposed to guard their homes."

"Against little kittens?" said Tex.

"Against anybody."

"Well, now you know we're your neighbours, you don't have to guard against us. We'd rather be friends."

"Me too," said the dog. "I haven't got any friends."

"I'm not surprised, if you go roaring and chasing after everybody in sight. What kind of a dog are you, anyway?"

"A Labrador," said the dog.

Sheelagh said to Tex: "What kind of cats are we?"

"We're Domestics," said Tex proudly. "I heard Moira telling Dick it said that on the vet's form Mrs Lynch gave them. She read it out: BREED: DOMESTIC."

"What did you say your names were?" asked the dog.

"Tex and Sheelagh."

"My name's Wolf. That's a fierce name. It's a good name for a guard dog. It puts off burglars."

"What are burglars?" Sheelagh asked.

Wolf explained that they were people who came into other people's houses when they weren't there, and took away their things. He was proud of how well he guarded the Rooneys' house, so that burglars were afraid to come in.

But it was a lonely life, Wolf said. The Rooneys were very nice, but he would love to have some animal friends too. He would have liked to find some dog friends, but there weren't many dogs around there.

"You're much better off having us cats as friends," said Tex. "We'll be a gang, the three of us."

"That's great," said Wolf.

"If we're a gang, you must let us into your garden," said Tex.

Wolf said they would be welcome to come in, any time. So Sheelagh climbed down from the platform, branch by branch. Tex climbed down after her. The dog and the two kittens greeted each other, touching paws to show they were friends, and in the same gang.

"I wish I could climb and jump like you," said Wolf. "I can't get out of this garden at all, except when they take me out for walks. Then they open that gate." He pointed to a wooden gate in the fence, and told them it could only be opened by a latch near the top, which he couldn't reach.

Tex and Sheelagh clambered up the tree and onto the fence, and walked along till they got to the gate.

"They twist that metal ring somehow," said Wolf, "and the latch goes up, and then they can open the gate."

Sheelagh looked down at the ring from their perch on the top of the gate. She reached down and grasped it in her front paws. Then, holding tight, she jumped, and hung from the ring, so that her weight pulled on it. The latch went up.

Wolf was jumping about excitedly. Now he pushed at the gate, and it opened. He bounded through it into the lane. Sheelagh and Tex went along the fence and got down onto the dustbin, and joined him.

Together, they wandered down the lane, sniffing at the smells. Before long, they heard an excited voice say: "Hey! It's Tex and Sheelagh!"

The kittens looked up. They saw two familiar figures gazing down at them from the top of a wall. They were Guinness and Butterscotch, their friends from the Cat Shelter.

They explained that some neighbours of Dick and Moira had heard how much they liked Tex and Sheelagh, and come to the Shelter to get two cats for themselves.

"You ought to be more careful about the company you keep!" warned Guinness, staring at the dog.

"Oh, this is Wolf," said Tex. "He's a friend. He's in our gang." Wolf wagged his tail vigorously. It made his whole body wiggle from side to side.

"How do you do?" said Guinness doubtfully.

"How do you do?" said Wolf.

"Can we join your gang too?" asked Butterscotch.

"Of course," said Tex. "The more, the merrier!"

Guinness and Butterscotch jumped down from the wall, and the five animals ambled down the lane, stopping occasionally to play chasing games.

When Tex and Sheelagh told them about their new home, Guinness nodded gloomily. "Just our luck!" he said.

"We aren't nearly as well off as you are. Our people put us out at night, and we have to sleep in a shed at the back of the house."

"That's tough," said Tex.

"I sleep outside too," said Wolf. "But I have a special kennel. They told me they put my name on it—WOLF."

"That must be so that none of the humans go to sleep in it by mistake," said Butterscotch.

As they reached the end of the lane, Tex and Sheelagh could hear roaring sounds—but they weren't the roaring of any kind of animal. They were like the sounds they'd heard when Mrs Lynch was bringing them to Dick and Moira's house. When the lane finished, they could see the metal creatures that were making the noise. They went rushing by at great speed, and gave out foul-smelling fumes.

"Cars," said Guinness. "People use them to dash from one place to another."

"Why can't they walk or run?" asked Sheelagh.

"They're too lazy," said Butterscotch.

"The cars only run on those hard grey paths they call roads," said Guinness. "Stay clear of them, that's my advice."

They sat at the end of the lane, watching the cars go by. Suddenly, Wolf stood up and cried: "Look! Across the road! It's Mrs Rooney, walking on the path!"

Before they could stop him, the dog ran out into the road. There was a screech of brakes, and a car skidded to a stop, only just missing the dog, which darted on across the road.

"Wolf! What are you doing out in the road?" Mrs Rooney was kneeling down, holding onto the dog, who was wagging his tail and licking her face.

A man got out of the car that had stopped and came across the road. He was very angry. "You ought to keep that dog under control!" he shouted. "He could have had us all killed!"

"I don't know how he got out," said Mrs Rooney.

Tex looked at Sheelagh and the others. "Don't say a word!" he said.

Guinness said: "You see what I mean about the cars? They're dangerous." After some more argument, the angry man got back into his car and drove away. Mrs Rooney came across the road, holding Wolf by the collar. At the entrance to the lane, she saw the four cats sitting watching.

Wolf smiled and wagged his tail.

"See you soon, Wolf!" said Tex.

"Now off you go up the lane," said Mrs Rooney to the dog. "I'll follow you and make sure the gate's shut after you. And don't you go chasing those cats!"

"Me? Chase cats?" said Wolf, looking at his four new friends. "What would I want to do that for!"

# 7

# The Birthday

Tex and Sheelagh saw the rest of their gang every day. They went into Wolf's garden and played chasing games. Once, Wolf fell into the pond and made a big splash, and one of the goldfish popped out onto the grass. Wolf stood in the pond gazing at it.

Sheelagh thought it might be good to eat, but Wolf asked her to put it back in the pond.

"The Rooneys seem very fond of those fish," he said. "I don't know why. Fish are very stupid. They swim round and round opening and shutting their mouths, without saying anything."

Sheelagh gave a flick of her paw, and the fish fell back into the pond with a plop. Wolf

climbed out, and shook himself, spraying Tex and Sheelagh with water.

Sometimes, when the Rooneys were out, Sheelagh did her trick with the latch of the gate, and let Wolf out into the lane. They played games there, and called to Guinness and Butterscotch to come and join them. Guinness usually did, but Butterscotch often just stayed on top of the wall, dozing.

"I have to save my energy," she said.

"For what?" Tex asked. "You don't do anything except sleep."

"I'm guarding," said Butterscotch. "If Wolf is a guard dog, why can't I be a guard cat?"

On wet days Tex and Sheelagh liked to keep Dick and Moira company in the room where they worked at their machines, writing. Tex liked to sit on Dick's shoulder, and watch the patterns of words appear on the screen as he tapped the keyboard.

If they were writing with pens instead of using the machine, Sheelagh liked to go and start a game, chewing at the pen. Or else she curled up and went to sleep on the piece of

61

paper they were writing on. Dick and Moira were kind: they didn't get annoyed. Instead they laughed, stroked Sheelagh for a while, and then lifted her off and put her down on the floor.

The first time Sheelagh was prowling around on the desk, there was a shrill ringing just beside her. She jumped into the air, and landed on the floor, near Tex.

"What was that?" she asked.

"They call it a telephone," Tex said. They watched Moira pick up the white thing that had made the noise. She started talking to it.

"Hello, Mother," she said. "How are you?"

"That thing can't be her mother!" said Sheelagh.

"No, it's a talking machine," said Tex. "It lets humans talk to each other when they're a long way away."

"Why can't they just shout?" asked Sheelagh.

"I don't know—perhaps the people are too far off. It does seem an odd kind of talking. After all, if *we* want to talk to Wolf, or Guinness and Butterscotch, we just go and see them. I suppose people are very lazy."

Sheelagh and Tex got used to seeing Dick and Moira talking to the white thing that sent their voices to other people. Moira talked so often to her mother, Sheelagh felt she knew the order of the buttons Moira pressed on the telephone. She could even have pressed them herself—but what could she say to Moira's mother, except "Miaow!"

The only room in the house where Tex and Sheelagh weren't allowed to go was the kitchen, where Dick and Moira got their own meals ready. When the kittens tried to help, by jumping up on the counter and poking around, they were always firmly picked up and put out of the room.

It puzzled Tex and Sheelagh that it seemed to take Dick and Moira so long to get these meals ready. And when they sat down to eat them, that took a long time too. Tex and Sheelagh could eat their own meal in two minutes, but Dick and Moira sat for an hour or more, pushing and cutting and spearing the bits of food on their plates, and then chewing them piece by piece.

They seemed to need special things to do this, called knives and forks and spoons.

"They are much less neat than we are," Tex explained. "I'm sure they would prefer to be like us, and just put the plate on the floor and kneel down and lick it all up."

On hot days, Dick and Moira used to go into their garden and sit at the table there, and read and talk. Sometimes they even took their meal out there. The first time they did that, Tex and Sheelagh thought it was an invitation to share the meal with them, and they jumped up onto the table and began to nibble. But to their surprise, Dick and Moira lifted them up and put them back on the ground.

One day when they were in the garden, Moira went into the house to answer the telephone. When she came out again, she told Dick: "That was Mother. She's asked us to come round on Saturday night for her birthday, and have dinner with her."

"Fine," said Dick. "We must think of a birthday present."

"Yes, I wonder what she'd like."

Sheelagh asked Tex what a birthday was. He said that people had some way of remembering the day they were born, and had parties on that day. It had happened once in the house he was in before. There was a girl there, called Jane, and on her birthday, lots of other girls came to the house in the afternoon, and ate and ate and ate, and played games, and squealed and shouted.

Jane was given birthday presents by the other girls, all wrapped up in paper, which she took off quickly to look at what was inside. Tex said he had great fun playing with the crumpled up pieces of paper, which he thought were much nicer than any of the things inside.

"Perhaps Moira's mother would like some crumpled up paper as a present," said Sheelagh, as they heard Dick and Moira still wondering what to give.

"Or maybe a toy mouse, like ours," said Tex.

"A *real* mouse would be even better," said Sheelagh.

They wandered across into Wolf's garden,

and told him about the birthday. Wolf said he thought a big juicy bone would be the perfect present for Moira's mother. Or perhaps a ball to run after. "We'll tell you what they decide when they go on Saturday," said Tex.

"I won't be here then," said Wolf. "That's the day I'm going on my holidays."

He explained that the Rooneys went for two weeks every year to the west coast, where there was a big beach to run about on, and water to splash about in and bark at.

"We stay in a hotel," said Wolf, proudly. "It's a big place, with lots of different rooms. It's a special hotel for dogs to go with their people. I remember the Rooneys talking about it. They said it says: DOGS WELCOME."

"Perhaps we may go to a hotel with Dick and Moira some time," said Sheelagh.

"I never heard of a hotel for cats," said Wolf. "I could ask around when I'm there."

"Thanks," said Tex.

On Saturday morning the gang all gathered in the lane, and said goodbye to Wolf and wished him a good holiday.

"We will come and sit on your fence, instead of our wall," said Guinness. "That way, we'll be guard cats for your house while you're away."

Wolf thanked them, and said goodbye and ran off when he heard the Rooneys calling him to get into the car.

Dick and Moira wrapped up the scarf they had chosen to give to Moira's mother, and said goodbye to the kittens.

"Have a nice quiet night," said Moira, as she closed the door.

But the night didn't turn out to be quiet at all …

# 8

## Unexpected Visitors

Tex and Sheelagh ate the dish of food that Moira and Dick put out for them just before they left. Then they prowled around the house for a while.

It was silent and still. The writing machines were off, so was the television. They sat down in front of the unlit fire.

"Let's go out!" said Tex. "We can see how Butterscotch and Guinness are doing as guard cats!"

They nosed their way out of the cat-flap and into their garden. There was a big moon in the sky, and the bushes cast shadows that moved in the light breeze. They heard an owl hoot in the distance, and a dog bark, far away.

They squeezed through the metal gate and into the lane.

They looked up at the fence on the other side. Two dark bulging shapes could be seen against the night sky.

Guinness and Butterscotch were lying on top of the fence.

They were fast asleep.

"We'll play a trick on them," said Tex. He went across to the dustbin a little way up the lane. It was made of metal, and the lid had been put loosely on the top. Tex stood on his back legs and nudged at the lid with his head. It slipped off the top of the bin and fell with a clatter to the ground.

"What's up?"

"What's the matter?" Guinness and Butterscotch woke up at once and sat up on the fence, looking around them wildly.

Tex and Sheelagh called: "Look out! Beware! Watch it! Run, run, run!"

Guinness and Butterscotch jumped off the fence and landed in the lane. They began to run, and bumped right into the kittens. All four

of them rolled on the ground. Tex and Sheelagh were doubled up with laughter.

"You're great guard cats!" said Tex. "You were fast asleep, the pair of you!"

"We weren't," said Butterscotch. "In any case, I can guard in my sleep."

"I don't think that trick was very funny," said Guinness grumpily.

"You should be guarding your own house, instead of playing jokes on us," said Butterscotch.

"Our people have gone out," said Sheelagh.

"All the more reason to guard," said Guinness.

Tex hadn't thought of that. "Perhaps you're right," he said.

So they said goodnight to Guinness and Butterscotch, who went back onto the top of the fence and lay down again.

As Tex and Sheelagh went through the cat-flap, they heard voices in the house. Dick and Moira must have come back. Perhaps they had forgotten something.

But why hadn't they switched on the lights? Tex and Sheelagh were about to rush to greet

Dick and Moira, when Tex put his paw up to hold Sheelagh back.

"Wait," he said. "There's something odd here." He remembered that there *had* been a light on—the table lamp that Dick and Moira always left on in the living-room.

Now the house was in darkness. Someone had turned it off.

They listened. Two men were talking to each other in low voices.

"Did you hear something?"

"No, what?"

"I thought I heard a clicking sound."

Tex realised it must have been the noise of the cat-flap opening and shutting when they came in.

"I can't hear anything," said the second man. "Shine the torch."

The door into the living-room was open. Tex and Sheelagh could see a beam of light. It moved around the room. They crept closer, hiding in the shadow underneath a table. Now they could see into the living-room.

In the torch-light they could see the shapes

of a small man and a big fat man. The small man was directing the torch beam around the room.

"There's a nice telly and a video over there," he said.

"And a cassette player in the corner," said the fat man. "We'll move them out into the hall, ready to hurry them out all together into the van."

"Let's see what else is here first."

They moved around the room, opening drawers and cupboards and looking on shelves.

"Who do you think they are?" Sheelagh whispered. "Perhaps they're friends of Dick and Moira's who called unexpectedly."

"Then what are they doing creeping about in the dark? No—I think they're burglars."

"Like the ones Wolf was talking about?"

"Yes, the people who come and take your things away."

Suddenly they heard the man with the torch say: "SSSH! Listen!"

"What's up?" said the fat man. "I can't hear a thing. You're getting too nervous for this job."

"It was a sort of a whining sound. Outside the door there."

The small man came to the door of the living-room. He shone the torch around. Soon the beam fell right on Tex and Sheelagh where they crouched under the table.

"Cats!" the small man snarled. "A pair of stupid cats!"

Tex and Sheelagh didn't know what the men might do to them.

They decided not to wait to find out. They darted across the room and plunged out through the cat-flap into the garden.

They stopped and hid in the shadow of a bush.

Through the glass of the back door they could see the two men come into the area where they had been, and shine the torch around. Were they going to hunt down Tex and Sheelagh?

The torch beam flashed towards the cat-flap, then moved away again, around the room. Tex and Sheelagh crept through the gate into the lane. The two shapes were still on the fence.

Tex hissed: "Guinness! Butterscotch! Wake up!"

"I wasn't asleep," said Butterscotch, yawning.

"Come down, please!" said Tex. "We've got burglars!"

Guinness and Butterscotch jumped down from the fence. Tex and Sheelagh explained what they had seen in the house.

"I wish Wolf was here," said Guinness. "Trust him to go off on his holidays just when he's needed!"

"Yes, he could have scared them off by barking," said Butterscotch. "People aren't scared of cats, no matter how much noise we make."

"We must think of some way to stop them, before they take all Dick and Moira's things," said Sheelagh.

"Maybe we could go back into our house," said Butterscotch, "and try and tell our people what's happening."

"They wouldn't understand," said Guinness. "They'd just think we were whining for more food."

"I wish we knew how to tell Dick and Moira, over at her mother's house," said Tex.

Sheelagh looked thoughtful. "Maybe there *is* a way we can tell them."

"But how?" Tex asked. "We can't go there. We don't know where Moira's mother lives."

"We don't have to go there," said Sheelagh excitedly. "We'll use the telephone!"

# 9

## Cat on the Phone

"The telephone?" Tex was amazed. So were Butterscotch and Guinness.

"Yes," said Sheelagh. "I've seen Moira phone her mother so often, I know the order of the buttons she presses."

"But even if it works," said Tex, "they don't understand what we say."

"We'll think of a way," said Sheelagh. "Come on."

They crept back in through the cat-flap. There was no sign of the burglars. They went into the hall, and saw the television and video, and the cassette player, piled up near the front door.

Then they heard voices from upstairs.

"Computers!" said the big man. "This is even

better than we thought. We'll get a good price for those."

"Right, let's unplug them and get them downstairs."

"Now's our chance," Sheelagh whispered. "They're out of the living-room now—we can use the phone in there."

The kittens ran into the living-room. The phone was on a small table beside the sofa. There was just enough moonlight coming through the curtains for Sheelagh to see the buttons on the telephone.

"Now let me think," she whispered. "What does Moira do first when she calls somebody?"

"She picks up that white thing and talks to it," said Tex.

"Right—you take one end and I'll take the other. We'll lift it off and put it on the table." When they had done that, they heard a faint noise coming from the phone.

"It's working," said Sheelagh.

She sat beside the telephone and slowly and carefully pressed the buttons in the order she remembered. They listened. From the phone

on the table they heard a new sound: a beeep-beeep, beeep-beeep, beeep-beeep.

"I wonder if they can hear?" said Sheelagh.

Then the beeep-beeep sound stopped, and they heard Moira's voice saying: "I'll see who it is, Mother. Hello? Hello?"

In the background there was the sound of a few people singing, "Happy Birthday to You."

"Let's miaow as loud as we can," said Sheelagh. Both the kittens leaned over the phone lying on the table, and miaowed.

They heard Moira say: "Sssh! I can't hear." The singing stopped.

Moira's mother called: "Who is it?"

Moira said: "This is very odd, but it sounds like cats. In fact it sounds just like Tex and Sheelagh."

The kittens were jumping up and down with excitement. They miaowed even louder.

Moira said: "It really does sound like them, but that's impossible. There must be something wrong with the phone. I'll hang up."

"She's going to go away!" said Sheelagh. "What shall we do?"

"I know," said Tex. He leaped onto a shelf where there was a vase of flowers. He pushed the vase over the edge. It crashed to the floor.

They heard Moira say: "Wait—I heard something else. Who *is* that on the line?"

Now Tex and Sheelagh heard other voices too, from the burglars upstairs.

"What was that? Go and have a look, while I start getting this computer downstairs."

There was a clatter of footsteps on the stairs. Tex and Sheelagh hid under the table, hoping the burglars would see the broken vase but not notice the telephone on the table. They were lucky.

The small man shouted: "It's only a vase, fallen off a shelf. Must be those stupid cats."

The big man was puffing and panting as he came down the stairs, carrying one of the machines. "Leave it," he called. "Give me a hand with this computer."

The small man went and took it from him, and carried it into the hall.

The big man said: "Now let's get the rest of the stuff from upstairs. Then we'll hunt round to see if there's any jewellery."

The two men went back up the stairs. Tex and Sheelagh jumped onto the table, and listened to the phone.

They heard Moira calling to Dick: "I heard two men talking about computers, and hunting round for jewellery. Dick—I think they're in our house. The cats somehow put the phone through to us."

They heard Moira's mother and Dick in the background, saying it couldn't happen. But Moira said firmly: "I know what I heard. And I'm going to phone the Guards right away. Then we must go home ourselves."

She hung up the phone. Sheelagh said: "They've cut us off, so they can phone the Guards."

She and Tex lifted the phone back into place.

They crept to the door of the living-room and peeped out. They could see the two burglars carrying the other computer down the stairs.

"Now, look in all the drawers and cupboards—there's bound to be some jewellery somewhere," said the big man.

"Why don't we just get out now, with this lot?"

"You're not scared, are you?"

"Of course not!" said the small man—but his voice sounded shaky.

They began to rummage in the cupboards and the drawers, first in the living-room, and then in the bedroom. The cats crouched in their hiding-place, waiting.

"I hope someone gets here quickly," whispered Tex.

"Yes, they'd better come soon," said Sheelagh, "otherwise those burglars will get away!"

# 10

## The Capture

The time seemed to go very, very slowly, as Tex and Sheelagh crouched there in the darkness.

From the bedroom they heard the big man say: "Right—I've found a couple of necklaces, and some fancy-looking ear-rings. I guess we've looked everywhere."

The small man said nervously: "I think we ought to get out of here."

Just then, the front door burst open with a crash. Tex and Sheelagh ran into the hall.

A man and a woman in Garda uniform were there. The man shone a big torch, but not quite in time to see the television and video piled on the hall floor with the cassette player and the computers. He tripped over them and cursed loudly.

The woman switched on the light and called out: "Who's there?"

The two burglars ran out of the bedroom in a panic.

The woman garda shouted: "Stop! We're the gardaí!"

The big man said to his mate: "Quick! Out the back way!"

They both rushed towards the back door. Sheelagh and Tex made a quick dash, and each grabbed the leg of one of the men, and dug their claws in. The men gave cries of pain. The big man lost his balance and fell down, and the small man tripped and fell on top of him.

Two more gardaí rushed in through the back door. They grabbed the men on the floor and held them down.

The first gardaí put handcuffs on them. The burglars got up, looking very gloomy indeed.

"That was a great tackle those cats did!" smiled the woman garda.

Tex and Sheelagh heard the voices of Moira and Dick at the front door. They came in and saw all the things piled up in the hall, then the gardaí and the burglars.

"I was right!" said Moira.

"You certainly were!" said Dick.

The gardaí told them how they'd found the lock broken, and the two men inside the house, getting ready to steal all their things.

"How did you know to call us?" they asked.

"We had a tip-off!" said Moira, looking fondly at the two kittens. "But if I told you who gave it to us, you'd never believe me!"

Tex and Sheelagh were the heroes of their gang. Butterscotch and Guinness loved to hear them tell the story of how they foiled the robbery. They told it again and again, and when Wolf came back from his holidays, they told it to him.

Wolf was full of praise for their bravery.

"You were almost as brave as dogs," he said. "What a pity I wasn't here, you could have called me and I'd have scared them off straight away."

"You couldn't use a telephone," said Butterscotch, "you're much too clumsy."

"Yes, the telephone was a neat trick," Wolf admitted. "That was clever of you, Tex."

"It was Sheelagh who did it," said Tex.

"Maybe there are other crimes we can solve," said Sheelagh.

"Yes," said Tex, "cats are so clever we could easily sort out a lot of things that puzzle the humans."

"We could set up as detectives!" Sheelagh was excited. "We could call ourselves CAT WATCH!"

A few days after the attempted robbery, Moira's mother came round for an evening meal. It was an extra birthday celebration, because the first one had to end so suddenly.

Moira and Dick made a new birthday cake too. They sang "Happy Birthday to You," and Tex and Sheelagh joined in, singing all the words. The others were delighted, although to them it just sounded like loud miaowing.

When Moira's mother cut the cake, she gave the first two pieces to Tex and Sheelagh.

"That's for the two cleverest cats in the world!" she said.

"Well, at least there are *some* humans who understand how clever we are!" said Tex, as they began to eat up the cake.

# THE JOKE THIEF

# 1

## The Cushion Game

When Dick put the cushion down on the floor, Sheelagh the kitten pounced on it. She began to wrestle with it, as if she was fighting another cat. This room was where Dick and his wife Moira worked. They were both writers, and the room had desks with word processors on them, and there were lots of books and shelves. But putting cushions on the floor was a new idea.

Dick smiled at Sheelagh's antics, and went downstairs. He came back with more cushions, and put those on the floor too.

"Tex! Tex!" Sheelagh called. "Come up here, Dick's invented a grand new game!"

All Dick heard was a series of miaows. People can't understand what cats are saying, though cats are able to understand human speech as well as their own.

"It's just one more way that cats are cleverer than people," Tex was always saying.

Now Tex bounded up the stairs and began wrestling with the cushions like Sheelagh.

"What's all that noise upstairs?" called Moira from below.

"The cats are attacking the cushions," said Dick. "They think I've put them there specially for *them*! Never mind, we can straighten them out later." He went downstairs again.

Sheelagh and Tex went on playing their fighting game with the cushions, until after ten minutes they got tired, and lay down.

"What did Dick mean?" asked Sheelagh. "The cushions *must* be specially for *us*. Who else could they be for?"

They heard the door-bell ring downstairs, and went down to see who it was.

"Hello, Mother," said Moira, opening the front door.

"Hello," said her mother. She glanced at the door, and said: "I'm glad to see you've got those strong locks on the door now, after the burglary."

"Yes, we're well protected now," Moira said.

"And thanks to these two kittens, the burglars were caught!" Moira's mother bent down and stroked Sheelagh and Tex. What she said was true: one night when Dick and Moira were at her mother's, two burglars had got into the house. Tex and Sheelagh had managed to press the telephone buttons to dial Moira's mother's number, and miaowed down the phone to let them know something was wrong. The guards had come and caught the burglars just as they were about to cart away the computers and the television set.

"We'll go out to the shops right away," Moira said. "The children will be here soon for Dick's first session."

"I'm not sure you're wise to let all those kids in to roam around the house."

Moira laughed. "There's only seven of them! And they won't be roaming around—Dick will be talking to them. The school asked if he'd give them some advice about writing. They want to start a school newspaper."

As Moira and her mother went out at the front door, Tex and Sheelagh went through the cat-flap at the back. They were looking for Butterscotch and Guinness, the cats who lived next door. The four of them had formed the Cat Watch Gang, and after they had made friends with Wolf, the dog who lived in the house at the back of them, they had let him join too.

Butterscotch and Guinness were asleep on the fence which divided Wolf's garden from the lane

behind Tex and Sheelagh's house. The kittens woke them up, and started to tell them about the children who were coming to the house. Wolf heard the cats talking, and came to the end of his garden to listen.

"Who are these children?" Butterscotch asked.

"They are coming from the school," said Sheelagh.

"Oh yes, that's where the children in our house go every morning," said Guinness.

"What do they do there?" asked Tex.

"I don't know exactly, but their mother is always shooing them out every morning, saying they mustn't be late."

"They bring things home from there too," added Butterscotch. "Those books they stare at, and pieces of paper too. After tea they sit at the table and make marks on them."

"That's called writing," said Tex.

"Could we learn to do it, if we went to school?" asked Sheelagh.

"Of course we could," said Tex, "but we don't need to. We can say all we want to by talking. People are not as clever as we are."

"Dick and Moira are writing all the time," said Sheelagh. "That's their job."

"What a funny job," said Guinness. "Our people both work in banks."

"Bottle Banks?" Sheelagh looked startled. "That must be very noisy, with all that glass crashing down all the time. Dangerous too."

"It's not that kind of bank," Guinness said. "As far as I can work out, it's a place where they give out money to people."

"They must be very kind," said Sheelagh.

"Mr Rooney at my house works in a garage," said Wolf. "He took me there once. People were crawling about all over cars and taking them to bits. It looked very clever. More difficult than writing."

"No, it's not," said Tex. He didn't like Wolf attacking Dick and Moira's work. "Our people write all kinds of things. Dick writes for one of those programmes on the television box people are always staring at."

"What sort of things does he write, then?"

"Funny things, they say. Jokes and such like. It's a programme for children."

"I don't know why people spend so much time staring at that box," said Butterscotch. "It's only a lot of lines and squiggles and colours. And the words that come out of it are dead boring."

Secretly, Tex agreed, but he defended Dick. "It's not all that bad..." he began.

Sheelagh interrupted: "Listen! I can hear people talking in our house. It must be those children Dick's going to teach writing to."

"Let's go and take a look," said Tex. "We'll see you all later." He and Sheelagh headed for the cat-flap and into the house.

# 2

## New Friends

The room was crowded. There were seven girls and boys standing around, while Dick talked to a small, round woman. No one noticed the kittens come in. They sat near the cat-flap and listened.

"I'll come back for them in an hour," said the woman. "I hope they'll have learnt something worthwhile from you by then."

"I'll do my best, Mrs Hogan," said Dick, smiling.

"Mind you, as a teacher, I don't really like the children watching television so much," said Mrs Hogan. "But the Head thought they'd learn something from you, so here they are."

"I think you can learn a lot from television," said Dick. "But in any case, I'll be talking to them about writing for the school newspaper they want to start."

"She was a bit rude to Dick, don't you think?" said

Sheelagh.

"Yes," said Tex. "She probably thinks she should be teaching them everything, and she's jealous of him."

"Look! Kittens!" cried one of the children. They had heard the miaowing conversation. Now several of them came over to Tex and Sheelagh and gazed admiringly. One girl knelt down and began to tickle Tex under his ear.

"Aren't you beautiful?" she said, as Tex started to purr. "What are their names?"

"That's Tex," said Dick, "and the black and white one is called Sheelagh."

"Hello, Tex, I'm Fiona," said the girl who was tickling him.

"And I'm Marian," said a girl with curly hair, stroking Sheelagh. "You're a lovely little pussy-cat, aren't you?"

"And I'm Seamus," said a tough-looking boy with red hair, "and I think cats are stupid."

"They're not!" said Marian. "They're brilliant!"

"Quite right," said Tex.

As Marian and Fiona went on stroking the kittens, everyone started arguing. They all defended cats except Seamus and a girl called Maureen, who said dogs were much nicer, especially her own dog, who was called Bran.

"Bran?" said Sheelagh to Tex. "Isn't that what Dick

101

and Moira eat for their breakfast?"

"Silence!" The sharp voice of Mrs Hogan cut through the noise. The chattering stopped. "Well!" the teacher went on, "I hope you'll all be a little quieter when the writing class begins."

She looked sternly at Dick, who said: "Yes, let's start, shall we? We'll go upstairs to the room where we work. See you later, Mrs Hogan."

Mrs Hogan said goodbye and let herself out at the front door. Dick went up the stairs, and the children followed. Seamus was last. He bent down towards the cats and said in a growling whisper: "Grrrr! Thick-heads!"

"Grrr, yourself, you ignorant idiot!" said Tex—but of course, Seamus only heard it as a rather sharp miaow.

"Let's go up and see what's happening," said Sheelagh.

The kittens padded up the stairs. There was an archway at the top, with no door. It opened into a big, bright room, with windows along one wall. Glass doors led out to a terrace where there were tubs of flowers. There was a long desk which stretched the length of the wall with the windows. At each end of the desk there was a word processor with a screen, and a chair in front of it.

Tex and Sheelagh sat on the top step of the stairs,

looking into the room. They saw Dick sit down in his chair.

"I hope you'll all be comfortable on those cushions," he said. The children found a cushion each and sat down.

"So that's what the cushions were for!" said Sheelagh. "Why can't they just sit on the floor like we do?"

"People are much more clumsy than cats," said Tex. "They can't fold up gracefully like we can."

"Now, first of all, I'd like all of you to tell me your names," Dick said. They each told him in turn. "And I'd like you just to call me Dick, this is a friendly session, not a school class."

He began to talk to them about the school newspaper, and the kind of things they could write for it. After a while, Tex began to yawn. He lay down on the step and was soon asleep.

Sheelagh went into the room. One or two of the children saw her, and smiled. Dick said: "It looks as if Sheelagh has decided to join us. I'm not sure quite what she will want to write for the newspaper, though."

There was laughter. "Maybe a Pets' Page," said Marian.

"Hey, that's a good idea," said Fiona. "We certainly ought to have a regular page about pets, giving advice and so on."

"Yes, that would definitely interest people," said Dick.

They went on talking about the Pets' Page. Sheelagh moved away and began prowling around the back of the room. She saw a cupboard with its door open a little way. She peeped in. Her nose twitched. There was a nice smell of some kind: a sweet, foody smell.

Sheelagh squeezed herself through the door. When her eyes got used to the gloom inside, she saw a tray. There were two plates on it. One was piled with biscuits, the other with pieces of cake. Sheelagh sniffed at the cake, but it was sticky. She turned to the plate of biscuits, and bit a piece off one of them. It was nice and crunchy. She settled down for a quiet snack.

It wasn't as quiet as she had meant it to be. She was just munching her third biscuit, when she heard voices nearby.

"It came from over here!"

"A sort of scrabbling sound—it's in that cupboard."

"Perhaps it's a mouse," said Seamus.

"That boy really is an idiot!" thought Sheelagh. "Imagine mistaking *me* for a mouse!" She poked her head out of the cupboard, just to show Seamus how wrong he was.

"Some mouse!" said a boy called Harry, and everyone laughed. Dick came over and tapped Sheelagh on the back.

"Out of there, Sheelagh," he said. "Those aren't meant for you." He looked into the cupboard. "Well, there'll still be plenty of biscuits and cake for you all later on. Now, let's get back to our paper."

They all sat down again, and Sheelagh crept across the room and back to the top of the stairs. Tex sat up and looked at her questioningly.

"What was that all about?" he asked. Sheelagh explained.

Tex chuckled. "Trust you to find where the food was!"

"It's my brilliant sense of smell," said Sheelagh. "None of those children knew there was food in that cupboard."

"People can hardly smell anything at all," said Tex. "You never see their noses twitching like ours."

The two kittens sat and listened as the session went on. People wrote things down on pieces of paper. Dick said: "Well, I think we're all agreed about what we should write, and next week we'll gather here again and read it to each other. Then we can start putting it on to the word processor and printing it out."

"Is that what you write your TV scripts on?" asked Harry.

"Yes, and my books and stories too," said Dick.

"Can we see what your TV script looks like?" said Fiona.

"Yes, if you like." Dick switched on the machine, and pressed a few keys. Some lines of letters appeared on the screen. "These are some jokes and riddles," said Dick. "They're for next week's programme."

The children crowded round, reading from the screen. They began to laugh. Dick was pleased.

"What was so funny about that?" asked Sheelagh, as Marian read out one of the riddles. "I could make up funnier jokes myself."

"So could I," said Tex.

"How about this?" said Sheelagh. "What did the cat say when they asked what she thought of the whole salmon she ate up from a dish in the kitchen?"

"What did she say?" asked Tex.

"She said it was *PURR*-fect!"

Tex laughed so much that he tumbled backwards and fell down several steps. He stood up, still laughing. Sheelagh bowed her head, to thank him for being such a good audience.

As Tex came bounding back up the stairs, he saw Dick and the children smiling at them.

"They find us very entertaining," said Tex. "You'd almost think they could understand the joke!"

# 3

## Cat Jokes

"Well, we'd better get back to work," said Dick, "we can't stand around watching the cats all day."

"I don't see why not," Sheelagh muttered.

Tex smiled. "Let's go down and tell your joke to the Gang."

They went down the stairs and out at the cat-flap. They found Butterscotch and Guinness in the lane. Guinness was trying to catch a butterfly. Butterscotch was dozing.

They told them the joke. Sheelagh was delighted when Butterscotch and Guinness laughed loudly. Then they heard a bark from the other side of the fence, where Wolf's garden was.

Sheelagh and Tex jumped up on the fence. Wolf gazed up at them. "What are you all laughing at?" he asked.

"I'll tell you," said Sheelagh. "Now, Wolf, what did the cat say when they asked what she thought of the whole salmon she ate up from a dish in the kitchen?"

"Wow!" said Wolf excitedly. "Did you really eat a whole salmon, Sheelagh?"

Sheelagh sighed. "No, Wolf, it's a joke question, see. You're supposed to ask 'What did she say?'"

"All right," said Wolf. "What did she say?"

"She said it was *PURR*-fect!" Sheelagh put out her paws, to emphasise the punchline. Tex jumped up and down with delight. Wolf just stood there, looking up at them with a puzzled expression.

Finally he said: "I don't get it."

"Whoever said dogs were intelligent?" Tex asked Sheelagh. He stared down at Wolf. "What sound do cats make when they're happy?"

Wolf thought for a moment. "Miaow!" he said.

"What *other* sound?" asked Sheelagh, trying not to sound impatient.

"Well, they purr, I suppose."

"That's right, Wolf, they purr. So it's funny when the cat says the salmon was *PURR*-fect. It means PER-fect, and PURR, like a cat."

Sheelagh thought the joke didn't seem so funny when you had to explain it. But Wolf gave a feeble laugh, still looking puzzled.

"*PURR*-fect," he said. "Very funny."

Just then, Mrs Rooney called from the house: "Wolf! Wolf! Din-dins!"

As Wolf turned and scampered towards the house, Tex said: "Why can't she just say Dinner?"

"Perhaps she thinks Wolf wouldn't understand."

"He probably wouldn't, judging by his reaction to your joke."

"Talking of dinner, I wonder if Dick's started giving out those biscuits yet."

When they reached the top of the stairs, the kittens saw that the biscuits had indeed been given out. The sounds of munching filled the room. Tex and Sheelagh wandered around, looking up with wide eyes and open mouths, as if they were about to fall down dead from hunger.

Marian gave Tex half of her biscuit, and Fiona gave Sheelagh half of hers.

"They shouldn't really eat between meals," said Dick, "especially as they already pinched a couple of biscuits from the cupboard."

"Well, they're not getting any of mine," said Seamus, cramming cake into his mouth.

The door-bell rang. "I expect that's Mrs Hogan, come to collect you," said Dick. "I hope you've enjoyed yourselves."

There was a chorus of thank-you's, as Dick led the way downstairs. Tex and Sheelagh followed. They perched on the window-sill and watched Mrs Hogan and the children go down the path, turning to wave to Dick.

Marian saw the kittens in the window, and gave a special wave to them. "See you next week, Tex and Sheelagh!" she called.

The children got into a blue mini-van which was parked outside the house. Mrs Hogan climbed into the driver's seat, and the van moved away.

"How lazy people are!" said Tex. "You'd think they could walk or run like us, if they want to go anywhere, instead of roaring about in those great things."

"Here's another of them," said Sheelagh. "The noisy one with two wheels and the boy with the red ball on his head."

A motor-cycle stopped outside the house, and the rider stepped off it. He took off his red crash-helmet and ran a hand through his long fair hair. The kittens watched him come up the path and ring the door-bell. As he waited for Dick to answer, he noticed Tex and Sheelagh in the window. He made a face at them.

Tex stuck out his tongue. The boy laughed. He was used to seeing the kittens. He was a messenger from the television station, and he arrived every week to collect Dick's script for the weekly show. They watched Dick hand the boy a big envelope, and say: "Thanks, Brian. Tell Jimmy Burke to ring me if he needs any changes."

"Sure thing," said Brian. He went back down the path, whistling.

"How *does* he do that?" asked Sheelagh. She had often tried to imitate Brian's whistle, but could only ever make a noise that sounded like hissing.

"It's a silly sound, anyway," said Tex. "I'm sure people only do it because they can't purr."

They watched Brian put the big envelope into the black box on the back of his motor-bike, and shut the lid. Then he put on his red helmet, climbed on to the saddle, and rode away.

"Those two-wheeled things make more noise than the big ones do," said Sheelagh.

"I think people who ride those, enjoy making as much noise as they can," said Tex. "Like Wolf, barking."

"Poor old Wolf," said Sheelagh, "he didn't get my joke at all."

"Dogs have no sense of humour," said Tex.

"I sometimes wonder if *people* have," said Sheelagh. "Dick does his best with those scripts he writes for that television programme, but honestly, I can't laugh at them like Dick and Moira do."

"We'll check out this week's, and see if it has got better," Tex said.

Two days later, Tex and Sheelagh sat in the middle of the room, as Dick and Moira settled down to watch the programme.

There were the usual shapes and colours on the screen, which Dick and Moira seemed to understand. A cheery young girl greeted the children in the audience, and began chatting away, interrupted every now and then by a squawking voice like a parrot, making remarks which everyone seemed to find funny.

Tex looked at Sheelagh to see what she thought. Sheelagh just shrugged, and raised her eyes.

Then a man with a loud voice started telling jokes and asking riddles. The children in the studio audience laughed a lot. Moira said: "They love it, Dick. And so they should, it's a very good script."

Tex and Sheelagh stared at the flickering screen,

listening intently. They still couldn't see anything to laugh at.

"Look at the cats!" said Dick. "You'd swear they could understand it all."

"If only they knew!" said Sheelagh. "Not only can we understand it, we could make up better jokes ourselves!"

"Let's do that!" said Tex excitedly.

"But how could we tell them to Dick?" Sheelagh wondered. "When we talk he only thinks we're making miaowing noises."

"I don't mean make them up for *him*! We'll make up a script for ourselves, and do our own show."

"Great!" said Sheelagh. "We'll call it THE CAT WATCH FOLLIES!"

# 4

## The Cat Watch Follies

Tex and Sheelagh ran out into the lane. They saw Guinness sitting on the fence, cleaning his paws with his tongue. Butterscotch was sleeping on the flat top of the shed which was just inside the fence, beside the gate.

The kittens jumped up on to the fence. Sheelagh said: "We've just had a wonderful idea! Butterscotch, wake up!"

Butterscotch woke and sat up, blinking. Guinness stopped cleaning himself and gazed at the kittens with interest. Eagerly, Tex and Sheelagh told them about their plans for THE CAT WATCH FOLLIES show.

"I've always fancied myself as an actor," said Guinness. "My grandmother was a Theatre Cat, you know. She used to sleep in a big basket where they

kept the costumes. One day the basket was sent on a train to a theatre in another part of the country. They were very surprised to see Granny when they opened it up!"

"What happened?" asked Tex.

"The theatre people were delighted. They were just going to stage a pantomime, called DICK WHITTINGTON, and they needed a cat to be in it. So Granny stayed there and performed every day. She was a big hit."

Sheelagh and Tex looked doubtfully at Guinness. Some of his stories sounded very far-fetched, but they didn't like to say they didn't believe him.

"Our show won't be a pantomime," said Tex.

"What will it be, then?" asked Butterscotch.

"We'll each take it in turns to do our own performances," said Sheelagh. "Tex and I can do jokes and riddles, as well as…let me see…as well as dancing."

Tex looked at her wildly. They had never done any dancing. But he said nothing. Sheelagh was clearly just making things up as she went along.

"That sounds great." Butterscotch was full of admiration. "What will you do, Guinness?"

"I'll recite a poem," said Guinness, "and I'll sing a song, too."

"What about you, Butterscotch?" Tex asked.

"Do I have to?"

"Of course. We're all in the show."

"Well...I could do an imitation."

"An imitation of what?"

"A statue. I could imitate a statue of a cat, sleeping."

The others stared at Butterscotch, who realised this idea wasn't much good. She added hopefully: "I could imitate a cat waking up too."

The others went on staring. Guinness broke the silence. "Butterscotch can join in my song."

"I've thought of something else," cried Tex. "We could do magic tricks. We could make Butterscotch vanish."

Sheelagh and Guinness looked at Butterscotch, who took so little exercise that she had grown quite fat. It was hard to imagine how she could be made to vanish.

Butterscotch couldn't imagine it either. "I don't want to vanish," she said.

"You don't really vanish, it's a trick," said Tex confidently, though really he had no idea how such tricks were done.

Just then, they saw Wolf ambling across the garden towards them. Excitedly, they told him about the show.

"Please, can I be in it?" he asked.

"It might be odd to have a dog in a show called CAT WATCH FOLLIES," said Guinness.

"It would be an extra attraction," said Sheelagh. "But what act could you do, Wolf?"

Wolf thought for a while. "I can do a Sit-up-and-Beg act," he said. "I can walk on my back legs too. And sing to the moon."

"I don't think singing is a good idea," said Sheelagh hastily. They had heard Wolf doing what he called singing at night, sometimes. It was more of a long, mournful howl than a song.

"Well, what about this?" said Wolf. "I could jump into the pond, then jump out and shake myself, and spray water all over the audience."

"No, definitely not!" said Tex.

"Well, then, what if you and Sheelagh climb on my back, and I trot around like a horse?"

"Now *that's* a good idea, Wolf!" said Sheelagh.

Guinness was frowning. "Wait a minute," he said. "I've just thought of something."

"What's the matter?" asked Tex.

"Wolf mentioned the audience," said Guinness. "We may get together a brilliant show, but there's no point in doing it if we haven't got an audience."

They all thought about this for a while. "What about Dick and Moira, and your people, Guinness, and the Rooneys from Wolf's house?" Tex suggested.

Sheelagh was doubtful. "I don't think people would understand what we were doing, any more than they understand what we say."

"No, they'd just think we were capering about, and screeching," said Guinness.

"I know what we'll do," said Tex. "A roof-top shouting session. At night, when lots of cats are roaming about. We'll all go to different roofs, and keep shouting: 'Roll up! Roll up! THE CAT WATCH FOLLIES are in town! Turn up in the lane behind Rooneys, two o'clock tomorrow!'"

"Fantastic!" said Sheelagh, and the others joined in to praise the idea.

"Now, let's all go off and practise our acts," Sheelagh said. "Then we'll meet here again tomorrow afternoon, and have a rehearsal."

In the living-room, Sheelagh sat in a chair, deep in thought. She was making up jokes and riddles for the show. In the middle of the room, Tex was practising a juggling act with a ping-pong ball. Then they worked out a dance. Sheelagh said if they moved forwards and backwards and sideways with the same paws at the same time, it would make a good dance. Then they could stand up with their front paws holding on to each other, and walk up and down. They would finish up by rolling on to their backs and kicking their legs in the air.

They tried it a few times, and were very pleased with themselves. Then Sheelagh noticed Moira at the door of the room, looking in. She was smiling. After a while, she went upstairs to the work room, and they heard her say to Dick: "Those cats are enjoying themselves. They're having one of their pretend fights."

Sheelagh snorted. "You see," she said. "I knew they wouldn't understand!"

The others were very impressed with Tex and Sheelagh's act the next day. They performed on the top of the shed, while the two cats and Wolf watched from the lane. They had used their trick of hanging on to the latch of the gate in the fence, to open it and let Wolf out.

First, Tex did his juggling, then Sheelagh told her jokes and riddles.

"What's the name of the cats' Father Christmas?" she asked.

"I don't know," said Tex.

"Santa CLAWS!" Butterscotch and Guinness laughed and repeated the words with delight. Wolf grinned a puzzled grin.

Tex and Sheelagh did their dance. It went very well, until they took too many steps to the side, and fell off the shed. Guinness and Butterscotch and Wolf laughed loudly. They thought it was part of the show.

Sheelagh winked at Tex and said: "They loved that. Let's keep it as part of the act."

Guinness and Butterscotch sang a song:

*There's a mouse in the house*
*And a cat on the mat*
*There's a dog on the log,*
*Now what do you think of that?*

Finally, it was Wolf's turn to do his trotting act. Tex and Sheelagh climbed up on his back, and he started prancing round in a circle. Then he stopped, so suddenly that the kittens fell off.

Standing staring at them, and seeming to block the whole width of the lane, was a huge Alsatian dog. Its teeth were bared in a snarl, and it looked as if it was about to spring.

# 5

## Basher Boris

The cats and Wolf froze. They knew if they moved, the dog would jump. They knew him, all right. He lived a few streets away, and his name was Boris. Everyone called him Basher Boris, because he went around fighting with every other dog he could find, and chasing all the cats in sight.

He didn't usually roam this far from his own area. In fact, his owners were supposed to keep him in, but they had a flimsy fence, and Boris was always bashing his way through it and going on a rampage.

"You bunch of whiskery wet lettuces!" Boris sneered. "Come out and fight!"

He stepped forward a pace. The others backed away. He stepped forward again, and they backed further. Step by step, he approached them, his head down, his lips dripping saliva, and his eyes blazing.

They backed away together, until they were against the wall of the lane. The cats would have jumped before, but they thought it safer to stay in a group, and they didn't want to leave Wolf on his own.

Now, with a great howl of rage, Boris sprang at them. They had no choice. The four cats leaped and scrambled up on to the fence, while Boris stood on his back legs, scratching at the fence and snapping at them.

"Come on up then, if you want a fight," said Tex boldly. He winked at Wolf, and gestured with his paw towards the gate. If they could keep Boris's attention on them, Wolf might be able to slink round the back of him and escape through the gate, into his garden. Wolf got the idea. Slowly he began to move, one step at a time. Boris went on snapping and snarling at the cats.

"Dogs don't know how to climb," said Guinness.

"Dogs don't know anything," said Butterscotch.

"What did the dog say to the tree?" asked Sheelagh.

"I don't know," said Tex.

"Don't bark at me!" said Sheelagh. The cats all laughed, and Boris snapped more furiously than ever. Wolf had nearly reached the gate, when Boris caught sight of him.

"STOP, YOU!" he shouted. Wolf froze. Boris went menacingly towards him. "And where do you think *you're* going?"

"N...n...nowhere," said Wolf nervously.

"Call yourself a dog?" growled Basher Boris. "I saw you, prancing around, playing with those kittens just as if you were some whiskered, whining furball, like them!"

"I know what we'll do," Sheelagh whispered to the others. "We'll pretend we're scared of Wolf." Then she said in a loud voice: "You're wrong, Basher! Wolf is real fierce. That's why he's called Wolf, you idiot!"

"Shut up!" snapped Boris.

"Yes, we're really afraid of him," said Tex. "He's only got to bark, and we run away in fright."

"Nonsense!" said Boris. "That dog is a wimp! He couldn't frighten a flea!"

"Don't you believe it," said Tex. He winked at Wolf again. Wolf began to bark loudly, looking up at the cats.

At once, they all gave a shriek, and climbed up on to the tree on the other side of the fence. They stood on the branches, pretending to whimper and shiver with fear. For a few moments, Basher stood there, wondering, and staring at the cats in the tree.

It just gave Wolf time to make a dash for the gate. He was back in his own garden! But Boris had seen him, and rushed towards the gate. Just in time, Tex and Sheelagh leaped down from the tree, and ran along the fence. Jumping on to the latch, they were able to click it shut, fastening the gate.

"OUUUUCH!" There was a howling cry of pain, as Basher Boris, at full gallop, crashed his head against the gate. He reeled back, stunned. He sat down, looking dazed, and wobbling a bit from side to side.

The cats sat in a row on the fence, smiling with victory. Wolf said: "Thanks, friends. Thanks a lot."

"You're welcome, Wolf," said Sheelagh.

"We couldn't let any harm come to a star of the show like you, could we?" said Tex.

Wolf grinned. Boris stood up and shook himself. He glared at the cats.

"Just you wait, you bunch of crawling cowards!" he said angrily. "One of these days I'm going to eat you for breakfast!" He went up to the gate and gave it a swipe with his right paw. Then he shouted at Wolf through the gate: "As for *you*, I'm going to smash you down and smear you all over the ground like a flea-ridden carpet!"

The big dog turned and walked slowly back down the lane.

"Goodbye, Basher," Tex called after him. "Have a nice day!"

Rehearsals went on every day, and there were no more visits from Basher Boris. But Wolf and the cats kept glancing down towards the end of the lane, just in case. They knew that Basher wasn't going to leave them alone for ever. He was the kind of dog that would try to take his revenge.

One day, Guinness was just finishing reciting his poem:

*...And so, the Giant Mice were beaten,*
*And every one of them was eaten.*
*The Champion Cat said: 'I'm the winner,*
*And now it's time I had my dinner!'*

Guinness bowed, and the others applauded. From inside the house, they heard a door-bell ring.

"That reminds me," said Sheelagh. "Today's the day those children come in for their writing lesson."

"We'd better go up and take a look at it," said Tex. "We might be able to give them some tips."

"And they might be able to give us some biscuits," Sheelagh whispered to him.

"See you later," Tex said, and the two kittens went in through the cat-flap.

This time they had no chance to get into the cupboard to get an advance bite or two of the biscuits. The cupboard door was firmly shut. So they sat on the top step, and listened, waiting patiently till biscuit-time at the end, when they were sure that Marian and Fiona would certainly share their biscuits with them.

The children had each done their writing for the newspaper. There were reports of football matches, and a story about a teacher who was given a secret powder in his drink so that he couldn't stop laughing. There was a description of a school outing to see a computer exhibition, a poem about turtles, and a Pets' Page about looking after cats.

They each read out their pieces, and then everyone discussed them.

The Pets' Page was Marian's. It was mainly about cats. "Not bad," said Sheelagh when she had finished. "But she might have said more about how clever we are."

"And how well we can sing." It was Guinness's voice. Tex and Sheelagh looked round, startled. Guinness and Butterscotch were sitting two steps below them on the stairs.

Tex grinned. "Welcome to the class," he whispered.

Just then, there was a loud howling sound from below, and a noise of snarling and barking.

"Help! Help!" They heard Wolf's voice, and all four cats hurled themselves down the stairs. Wolf's head and front legs were poking through the cat-flap. He had wandered after Guinness and Butterscotch, to see what was happening indoors. But he was too big to get through the gap, and now he was stuck.

And behind him, outside in the garden, was Boris, snarling with furious pleasure, as he sank his teeth into Wolf's tail.

# 6

## The Dog in the Cat-Flap

"What's going on?" cried Dick, coming downstairs after the cats. The children began to follow him, crowding on to the stairs to peer down at the rumpus below.

"Look, there are four cats now!" said Fiona.

"And a dog!" said Marian.

"It's poor old Wolf, from the Rooneys' house at the back," Dick said. "I wonder how he got out. And who's that other dog?" He looked out of the window. Then he banged on it. Boris let go of Wolf's tail and backed away a few steps. He stood there, barking loudly.

Dick tried to ease Wolf back out of the cat-flap, but he was too firmly stuck.

"We've got to get Boris away from him," said Tex.

"We can't get out, the cat-flap's blocked," said

Guinness.

"Come on, the kitchen window's usually open," said Sheelagh. Soon they were out in the garden. They began darting at Boris, nipping his paws and his tail, and rushing away. Boris whirled around in circles, trying to snap at them, but they were always too quick for him.

Then Tex said: "I'll try and lure him away." He jumped on to Boris's head and dug his claws into his neck. Boris gave a yelp of pain, and twisted his head round. Tex jumped down, and ran through the gate and down the lane. Boris was so angry with him that he followed him out.

Tex hurried down the lane with Boris bounding after him. Just as the big dog reached him, he leaped up on to the wall. Boris stood below, scrabbling at the wall with his front paws and barking wildly.

Meanwhile, in the garden, Sheelagh, Butterscotch and Guinness were trying to help Wolf by pulling at his back paws and his tail. But they didn't want to take too firm a grip with their teeth in case they hurt him, so they kept losing their grasp and stumbling backwards. Dick was still trying to push from the other side of the cat-flap, helped by Marian and Fiona.

It was hard to open the door because of the cat-flap in it, with Wolf stuck there. But they eased it open a little, and Harry and a girl called Catherine came out into the garden and began pulling at Wolf. The whole scene looked like a tug of war.

Then Sheelagh had an idea. "You know when we cats stretch out on the rug in front of the fire?" she said to Guinness and Butterscotch. "It makes our shape long and narrow, doesn't it?" The two cats agreed. "Well, if Wolf stretched out, instead of being pushed and hunched up, maybe he'd be narrow enough to slip back through the flap."

"Good thinking, Sheelagh," said Guinness. They jumped back through the kitchen window. At the cat-flap on the inside, Dick was patting and reassuring Wolf, before trying another push.

"We've got an idea, Wolf," said Sheelagh. "Try stretching your front legs forward as far as you can, keeping your head forward too."

Wolf did what she said. Instead of bunching up, his shoulders were now stretched out. When Harry and Catherine gave their next pull at his back legs, his body slid back through the gap. He collapsed in a heap in the garden, and Harry and Catherine let go and staggered backwards.

Dick opened the door and came out, followed by the cats and the children. They all crowded round Wolf, who got up and shook himself, wagging his tail.

"Thanks a lot, Sheelagh!" he said. He looked around

and asked: "Where's Tex?" Down the lane they could hear the barking and growling of Basher Boris.

"He lured Boris out of the way," said Sheelagh. "Now we must go and help him."

They all went out into the lane, followed by Dick and the children.

"Look!" said Marian, "that horrible dog is snapping at Tex, on the wall."

"Let's go get him!" said Fiona. The cats and the children, in one big stampede, went pounding down the lane, shouting and giving war-whoops. Boris stopped barking and looked round.

"Boris, your time has come!" cried Sheelagh. "Cats to the rescue!" Boris looked alarmed. He began to back away down the lane as the mob of children and cats came hurtling towards him. As they caught up with him, he put his tail between his legs, and turned and ran.

As he disappeared into the road at the end of the lane, Tex jumped down from the wall.

"Good work, Tex!" said Sheelagh.

"It was nothing," said Tex casually. "After all, he's only a dog." Then he noticed Wolf. "No offence meant, Wolf!" he said.

"None taken," said Wolf, smiling.

In the following days, Wolf and the cats went on

practising for the CAT WATCH FOLLIES show. They were so keen to get it right, and concentrating so hard on rehearsals, they even forgot to go and listen in to the next writing session, but stayed out in the lane instead.

They suddenly realised they had missed the session, when they saw Dick and some of the children in the garden at the back of the house.

"I'm sure they're out here somewhere," they heard Dick say.

"We'd love to say hello to them before we go," said Marian.

"There they are!" said Fiona, spotting Tex and Sheelagh doing their dance on the roof of the shed. "They're playing!"

"And there are the other cats and that dog, in the lane," said Catherine.

They all came out into the lane. Tex and Sheelagh jumped down off the shed. The children patted them, and they patted Guinness and Butterscotch and Wolf too.

"I wonder who left Wolf's gate open," said Dick. Tex and Sheelagh smiled. "You'd better go back in, Wolf," Dick went on. "The Rooneys will be wondering what's happened to you." He took Wolf gently by the collar and led him to the open gate. Wolf wagged his tail, barked a goodbye to the cats, and went into his garden. Dick closed the gate and the latch clicked shut.

"We'd better get back inside," said Dick. "Mrs Hogan will be coming to collect you soon."

From their position on the window-sill, Tex and Sheelagh watched the van drive away. Soon afterwards, Brian rode up on his motor-bike. Dick gave him the latest script and he stowed it in the box on the back of the bike, climbed on and rode noisily away.

"It's a pity Dick's audiences can't see *our* show," said Tex.

"Or hear it, at least," said Sheelagh. "If we could get them to put it on that radio thing Dick and Moira listen to, then all the cats would be able to hear it."

"We'd be national stars!" said Tex.

"Think of it—THE TEX AND SHEELAGH RADIO SHOW."

"The Cat-Show Chat-Show!"

"There's only one problem," said Sheelagh. "Even if we could get the radio station to let us do it, the people listening would only hear half-an-hour of miaows and purrs."

"That would be better than some of the boring talk they hear already."

"That's true. When we've done our show for the cats, we'll work out a radio version of it."

That evening, as the two kittens were lying on their chair, dreaming of radio stardom, the phone rang and Dick went to answer it. They woke and sat up as they heard him talking in startled, anxious tones.

"But it can't be! I haven't even seen the paper...Jimmy, you know I wouldn't do that...All right, we'll talk about it tomorrow."

Dick came back into the room. He looked very pale.

"I can't believe it, I just can't believe it!" he said, his voice shaking.

"What's happened?" asked Moira anxiously.

"That was Jimmy Burke, the producer of the TV programme. He's just read the script I sent in today. He says that two of the jokes were in the Children's Page of one of the papers, and he thinks I must have copied them!"

139

# 7

## The Joke Thief

Dick paced about the room, twisting his hands together. "It's impossible! Impossible!" he kept saying.

Moira said: "Well, of course it is. You'd never steal jokes from somewhere else. Jimmy Burke knows that."

"He didn't sound too sure, on the phone. Imagine him thinking that. Me, a Joke Thief! It's ridiculous."

"What paper was it in?"

"The *Trumpet*. They give two pounds for every joke or story they print."

Sheelagh said to Tex: "Someone must have stolen the jokes from Dick and put them in the paper."

"Who could it be?" asked Tex.

Dick and Moira were asking themselves the same question. Moira said: "It must be somebody in the TV station. Someone who saw the scripts beforehand."

"That's a lot of people," said Dick. "The typists, photocopy people, actors, designers...It could be anybody. Yet I know most of them, and nobody would do a thing like that."

"Perhaps you're too trusting," said Moira.

"He's much too trusting," said Tex. "We must suspect everybody."

"And we must help Dick find the Joke Thief," said Sheelagh.

"How?"

"I don't know yet, but we'll think of something. After all, we caught those burglars, didn't we?"

"Perhaps it's them again," said Tex.

"Or different ones," said Sheelagh. "Burglars who like jokes. I know what we'll do. Instead of sleeping in our chairs downstairs tonight, we'll keep guard up in the work-room, where Dick keeps his scripts. If anybody creeps in to steal them, we'll raise the alarm."

They went up the stairs. The work-room was quiet, and lit only by the moon beaming through the windows.

"Look!" said Tex. "The drawer of that cabinet is open. Perhaps the thief has been in already!"

"Maybe Dick left it open himself—let's hope so. It's very careless, though. But it gives us a chance. The burglars mustn't see us lurking. If you hide over in the shadows under the desk there, I'll get into the drawer of the cabinet with the scripts. When the Joke Thief reaches in, I'll bite his hand! Then you can run down and alert Dick and Moira."

"Brilliant!" said Tex. He crept into the darkness under the desk. Sheelagh climbed into the drawer, where there was a gap behind the row of scripts in cardboard folders. She crouched down and waited.

She didn't have to wait long. After a few minutes, they heard footsteps coming up the stairs. The light went on. It was Dick. They heard him call down to Moira: "I'll just make sure everything's all right up here."

From her hiding place, Sheelagh heard him approach the cabinet. He muttered: "Well, I suppose I'd better lock that drawer, just in case!"

Then he shut the drawer, turned the key, and walked away. Sheelagh was in complete darkness. She felt stifled by the narrow space. She wondered if she would be able to breathe till she was let out, or would the air be all used up?

She began to miaow, but no one seemed to hear. Tex came to the rescue. As Dick turned out the light and began to go downstairs, Tex jumped out from his hiding place, and made loud, frantic yowling sounds.

Dick stopped. "Hello, Tex. What are you doing up here? What's the matter?"

Tex grabbed the bottom of Dick's trouser-leg and began to try to pull him in the direction of the cabinet.

"No, no, Tex, let go," said Dick. "We're not playing games just now."

"Games!" thought Tex. "People are very thick sometimes." He went on alternately tugging at Dick's trouser-leg, and mewing and yowling. Dick looked puzzled. Then Tex dashed across to the cabinet. He stood on his back legs, and began drumming his front ones against the drawer where Sheelagh was trapped.

Dick knew that usually the only time Tex did that was against the kitchen door, when his food-bowl was being got ready inside.

"There's no food in there," said Dick. But as Tex went on drumming and mewing, Dick went over to the cabinet. "Look, I'll show you," he said. He unlocked the drawer and opened it.

He staggered back in surprise, and Sheelagh leaped out with a cry of relief. "However did you get in there?" Dick asked. "If it hadn't been for Tex, you'd have been there all night." He patted the two kittens.

"Thanks a lot, Tex," said Sheelagh. Dick locked the cabinet again, turned off the light, and went downstairs. The cats sat down to wait again, both of them together this time in the darkness under the desk.

An hour went by, then another. They both felt their eyelids drooping. Before long, they were asleep.

They were woken by the sound of a crash. It came from outside on the terrace.

"The burglars!" cried Tex. They both rushed to the window and peered out.

In the moonlight, on the terrace, they saw that a big plant-pot had been knocked over. Sitting nearby, looking at it, were Butterscotch and Guinness. Tex tapped on the window with his paw. The next-door cats looked up.

"What are you doing?" Tex shouted.

"We were rehearsing a dance number to put in the show," Guinness shouted back. "I started dancing on that flower-pot, and it fell over. They should make those things more solid."

"We thought you were burglars," called Sheelagh. The light went on. Dick came up the stairs. He peered out of the window, then opened the door and went out on to the terrace. Tex and Sheelagh followed. Dick saw the overturned flower-pot, and the cats beside it.

"Oh, it was *you*, was it?" he said. "Well, that's a relief." He tipped the pot upright again.

"That's enough rehearsing for tonight," Sheelagh whispered to Guinness. "Let's see the dance tomorrow."

Tex and Sheelagh went on with their burglar-watch in the work-room. This time they decided to stay awake in turns, for half-an-hour each. Nothing more happened. Sheelagh was on watch, when the dawn came up and the sky got light. Birds started singing. From the road, she could hear the noise of a few cars and motor-bikes.

Suddenly she had an idea. "Tex, Tex! Wake up!" she called. "I think I know who the Joke Thief is!"

# 8

## Dangerous Journey

"Who is it?" asked Tex eagerly.

"Well, who would get a chance to have a look at the scripts on his own, before anyone in the TV station sees them?"

Tex thought for a moment, then said: "Brian! The boy on the motor-bike who collects the scripts from Dick."

"Exactly!" said Sheelagh. "He could stop on the way to the TV station, in some quiet spot, read the scripts, and copy the jokes."

"It seems very likely it's him," said Tex. "But how can we prove it? We'd have to catch him doing it."

"We must try to think of a way."

They both sat thinking, while the day got brighter outside. Then Tex said: "I've thought of a plan. It's risky, but it just might work..."

After the next writing class, the children gathered downstairs to play with the cats, while they waited for Mrs Hogan to collect them. This time, when the children trooped out of the front door to get into the waiting van, Tex and Sheelagh didn't go to their usual place on the window-sill to watch. Instead, they slipped out of the front door and went and sat under a bush near the path.

The van moved off, and before long, Brian's motor-bike roared to a halt outside the front gate. He took off his red helmet, smoothed his hair, and walked up the path. He rang the door-bell and waited.

"Now's our chance!" said Tex. They slipped out on to the path, and through the gate. Tex jumped up on the saddle. With his paw, he pulled at the lid of the box on the back of Brian's bike. It flipped open. There were some papers inside.

"In we go!" called Tex. Sheelagh jumped up beside him, and they both got into the box. They burrowed underneath the papers and lay still. They heard Brian saying goodbye to Dick, and then the front door closing.

Brian came towards them down the path, whistling. As she often did, Sheelagh tried to imitate the sound, but all that came out was a hiss. Tex whispered: "Sssh! He'll hear you."

They heard Brian stop beside the bike. "That's odd," he said. They realised he had seen that the lid of the box was open. Then he said: "It must have blown open, I guess." He put the envelope down on top of the other papers. The kittens held their breath. Would he notice that the box seemed fuller than before?

But then they heard the lid shut. He hadn't discovered their hiding place. With a loud roar, the motor-bike started.

Tex and Sheelagh began the most uncomfortable journey they had ever made in their lives.

The box shook and rattled and swayed as the motor-bike went speeding along the roads. The kittens were flung from side to side. When the bike went over a bump in the road, they hit their heads on the lid. They were afraid it would fly open and they would be flung out. But luckily, Brian had fastened it firmly shut this time.

Finally the bike stopped. "Maybe this is when he'll take the script out and copy the jokes down," said Sheelagh.

Indeed, Brian opened the lid of the box, and took out the envelope. But he didn't wait to open it. He walked away, whistling. Tex pushed his head upwards. The catch was off the lid again, and he was able to raise it a little. The kittens peered out through the gap.

They saw Brian walk up a short, paved pathway and through some glass doors in a big building. "That must be the TV station," said Sheelagh.

"He didn't stop to look at the script. It must be somebody else, after all."

"If we could get into the building, perhaps we could find out who."

"I'm afraid they would just turn us out," said Tex. "They don't realise we're intelligent, and could put on just as good a show as they do."

"Better!" said Sheelagh.

"I've just thought of something," said Tex, in a worried voice. "How are we going to get home?"

"I don't know," Sheelagh said. "We can't stay hiding in here, till Brian goes back next week for another script from Dick."

"We'll have to find our own way back."

"How do we do that? We don't know where we are. Or which way home is."

Tex said: "I remember Dick and Moira talking about some story they saw on the TV box. It was about some animals that were lost, and found their way home over miles and miles of snow and forest. Somehow they knew which way to go. If we just got out of this box and set off, maybe we would know too."

"It's worth a try," said Sheelagh. "Perhaps we could get a ride on that green train we can see from the roof of the house."

"Or we could get on a bus. If they let cats on."

"They certainly ought to. There should be special seats reserved for us. Meanwhile, let's get out of here, anyway."

They pushed the lid open and jumped to the ground. In front of the building there was a road, with cars parked on each side of it in rows.

"They must belong to the people who work here," said Sheelagh.

The road led down to a big gateway. The kittens decided to make their way to it. They walked along beside the road, shrinking away from the cars that came past them with a deafening roar, their wheels only a few centimetres away from them.

Soon they were outside the gateway. Here there

was a much bigger road, and the traffic was much faster and much louder. Cars, trucks and vans were rushing by, in a never-ending procession. The fumes from them smelled dreadful. "Which way now?" asked Tex. "Have you got any feeling where home is, like the animals in the story?"

Sheelagh put her nose in the air, and sniffed around. Then she sighed. "I haven't a clue," she said.

"Nor have I," said Tex.

"If we go into that road, a car might flatten us. You remember what happened to that poor old cat down the street." They both shivered.

"If we climb up on that stone pillar beside the gate, perhaps we could see something which would give us an idea," Tex suggested. They jumped up. At least they felt a bit safer here, and they were away from the fumes at ground level.

They looked around. They could only see the road, and buildings, and more buildings. There was a tall metal mast stretching up into the sky, just in front of the TV station building. "Maybe we should climb up that," said Sheelagh.

They looked up at it. It was taller than any of the buildings—four or five times as tall as the TV station. And the top of it seemed to sway to and fro, against the clouds high up in the sky. It made the kittens giddy just to look at it.

They heard the roar of a motor-bike, coming towards the gate. The rider had a red helmet. "It's Brian!" cried Sheelagh. "He's our only chance!"

"You're right," said Tex, as Brian came up to the gate. Just outside it, he stopped, waiting for a gap in the traffic so that he could join the big road.

"Jump!" they both cried together, and leaped into the air.

# 9

## The Trap is Set

They landed, one kitten on each of Brian's shoulders. He got such a shock, that he and the bike fell over. There was hooting as a car just behind him stopped suddenly. Brian got up, righted the bike, and moved it to one side. The car went past.

The kittens had jumped away, and were now sitting on the ground, looking up at Brian. At first he looked puzzled, but then he recognised them. "How on earth did *you* get here?" he said in surprise.

Tex jumped on to the box at the back of the motor-bike and tapped the lid with his paw. Brian looked even more surprised.

They heard him mutter to himself: "I must be going barmy—for a moment, I thought he understood what I said! They must have got into the box, and I drove off without realising they were there."

Sheelagh jumped up beside Tex. They both began miaowing in a pleading way. "Well, I can't leave you here," said Brian. "I suppose I'd better take you back. Come on, in you get!" He opened the lid of the box and the two kittens scrambled in. Brian closed the lid and made sure it was firmly shut. The bike roared to life.

The journey back was as bumpy and lurching as before. When they got home, Tex and Sheelagh jumped out as soon as Brian opened the lid. They ran up to the front door. Brian followed, and rang the bell.

The reunion was joyful. Dick and Moira thanked Brian again and again, and they all had a drink to celebrate the kittens' return. Dick and Moira had been very worried about them, wondering if they had strayed into the road and got run over, or Boris had attacked them and they were hiding somewhere in fear.

Dick and Moira had gone up and down the road, calling the kittens' names, and they had done the same thing in the lane. There, Butterscotch and Guinness were sitting on the fence; they had begun to worry about Tex and Sheelagh too. They were delighted to see them back, and the kittens told them all about their adventure.

Butterscotch and Guinness showed them the dance

they had been practising the night they knocked over the flower-pot. "That's great!" said Sheelagh. "We must definitely have it in the show."

"When are we going to do the show?" asked Guinness.

They all talked about it, and decided to do it the following week, on the day Dick had his writing class. Moira was always out with her mother then, and Dick would be inside concentrating on the class. The Rooneys were out all day too, so there would be no people about to see the large audience of cats in the lane, watching the performers. Tex and Sheelagh knew that people wouldn't understand what was going on, and might object to a whole mob of strange cats milling about.

They decided to start advertising the show that very night. So at midnight, they went along the rooftops, calling out: "It's here! The show you've been waiting for! THE CAT WATCH FOLLIES SHOW! Coming in seven days time, two o'clock, in the lane. BE THERE!!"

It was a busy time for the cats. They spent a lot of the day rehearsing, and every night they went out on the rooftops to shout about the show. Now and then, a window was thrown open and a head peered out, and someone yelled at the cats to be quiet. Once a particularly angry person even threw a shoe at Tex.

He ducked just in time. Sheelagh said: "How rude! But they'll be sorry in the morning, when they have to go out and hop down the street on one foot!"

The mystery of the Joke Thief was still unsolved. But no more of Dick's jokes had appeared in the paper. Dick and Moira wondered if it could have been just some kind of coincidence.

Then, the day before they were due to do THE CAT WATCH FOLLIES show, Dick got another phone call from the producer Jimmy Burke. He had been sent a copy of a country paper several days old, by his brother, who thought he'd like to see a mention of Jimmy in the TV column.

But looking through the paper, Jimmy had also seen an item called *Just for Laughs*. It was a batch of jokes, sent in by readers, and among them was one which had been in the most recent script Dick had sent in.

Dick was very upset. He told Moira: "I think Jimmy realises I couldn't have seen that paper and pinched the joke, but he wonders how someone could have pinched it from *me*. He said I must be careful who I show my scripts to."

"But you don't show them to anyone, except me," said Moira.

"I know—I can't understand it. But it's certainly not helping my reputation at the TV station. They might even fire me if it goes on."

Tex and Sheelagh heard this. They decided that the mystery must be solved. They talked long into the night about it.

"We know it's not Brian, anyway," said Sheelagh. "And we've been guarding the upstairs, so we know no burglars have broken in."

"In any case, Dick has been locking the drawer with the scripts in it," said Tex.

"Wait a minute!" said Sheelagh. "That isn't the only place the jokes are in!"

"Where else are they?"

"In that machine on the desk, with the keyboard and the screen. The one he sits tapping away at. He makes up the jokes and the rest of the script on that, then puts it on to the paper with that printing machine."

"So someone who knew how to do it could make the jokes come up on the screen!" cried Tex. "But nobody goes near that machine except Dick and Moira."

"Oh yes, they do," said Sheelagh. "Every week."

"The children in the writing class!" said Tex.

"Exactly!" said Sheelagh.

"But Dick's always there with them."

"Not the whole time," said Sheelagh. "Not at the end of the class. Remember that day when Wolf got

160

stuck in the cat-flap and we all rushed down to help him. I don't think all the children came down."

"You're right," said Tex. "Come to think of it, I can't remember seeing that boy they call Seamus with the rest of them."

"And he was the last down, another time, too."

"So you think he stayed behind and got at the keyboard, and got the jokes on to the screen, and wrote them down?"

"It certainly explains a lot. He could have sent the first two to the paper with the Children's Page, before Dick sent in his script to that producer. The same the next time, only then he sent them to a different paper, in the country, probably in a place he knows."

"The class is coming tomorrow. We must warn Dick," said Tex.

"He can't understand us," said Sheelagh. "Oh, I do wish sometimes that people were more intelligent! No, what we'll have to do is catch him in the act."

"We can't be there checking up on the class tomorrow. It's the day of the show. And we can't cancel it, the audience will be turning up in the lane at two, and if we say there's no show, there'll be a riot."

"The class will be ending about the same time as the show. We'll have to arrange the acts near the end so that you and I can take it in turns to go and keep an eye on Seamus. That's the time he'll try to get at the machine."

"I hope the scheme works."

"It's got to work! The Joke Thief must be caught!"

# 10

## Show Business

Tex and Sheelagh walked up and down the fence, calling out: "Roll up! Roll up! Take your places for the show of a lifetime, THE CAT WATCH FOLLIES!"

Behind the fence, in Wolf's garden, Guinness, Butterscotch and Wolf peered through a crack at the scene in the lane. One by one, cats began arriving. There were black cats, tabby cats, ginger cats, and striped cats. There were fat cats, thin cats, handsome cats and scruffy cats. There were large cats, small cats, short cats and tall cats.

"It's going to be a big audience," said Guinness.

"I'm so nervous!" said Wolf, in a shaky voice."I've never been in a show before."

"Nor have any of us," said Butterscotch.

On the fence, Tex said to Sheelagh: "What a great crowd! There must be fifty cats at least." They gazed

down on the audience below. Some of the cats were sitting staring up at them. Others were curled up, asleep. Many of them were chattering to each other, wondering what the show would be like.

A mischievous little black-and-white cat was going up behind the sleeping cats, and giving their tails a nip, and then running away. Two big fluffy Persian cats were arguing about which were the best seats. A slinky Siamese decided the best viewpoint was up in the tree, so she climbed up there, and several of the others followed.

Then a burly brown cat, with fur that stuck out all round his face, began to chant: "Why are we waiting?" Some of the others joined in.

Tex said to Sheelagh,"I think we'd better begin." They both shouted together: "Welcome! Welcome! Welcome! Welcome everyone, to the famous, amazing, altogether mega-brilliant CAT WATCH FOLLIES SHOW!"

Down below, Guinness said to Butterscotch: "That's our cue—we're on stage!"

"Good luck!" said Wolf, as his two friends leaped up to join Tex and Sheelagh on the roof of the shed. The four cats lined up in a row, stepping along the shed roof and back, in time with each other, and waving their tails in the air, as they sang:

*The Cat Watch Follies are really a wow,*
*The Cat Watch Follies are taking a bow,*
*So all together, join in with us now,*
*And cheer us along with a big MIAOW!*
*Miaow, Miaow, all together now,*
*Cheer us along with a big MIAOW!*

They repeated the chorus, and many of the audience joined in. At the end of the song and dance, there were cheers and shouts of "More! More!"

The four cats bowed. "They loved us!" said Sheelagh to Tex. "We're a hit!"

The show went on, and the audience were delighted with every number. They fell about laughing at Sheelagh's jokes and riddles. They tapped their paws in time to the dances. Guinness and Butterscotch's dance was a great success, and they did it twice. The second time, Butterscotch was so carried away with her success, that she gave a final leap into the air and fell off the roof, into the audience.

Tex juggled with his ping-pong ball, Guinness did his recitation, and as the grand finale, they lifted the latch of the gate, and Wolf came trotting out. Tex and Sheelagh jumped down on to his back, and he moved up and down the lane, among the audience, who laughed and applauded and cheered. They were pleased and astonished to see a friendly dog in a show for cats.

As Wolf trotted around, Sheelagh said to Tex: "It must be getting near the end of the writing class. Why don't you do a bit more juggling, while I go up and take a look at what's happening?"

"Right!" said Tex. But before he had time to do any juggling, there was a barking roar from the end of the lane, and a huge, snarling, lumbering figure came rushing towards them. It was Basher Boris.

He dashed into the midst of the crowd of cats, barking fiercely and snapping with his huge teeth. "Beware of the Dog! Beware of the Dog!" shouted Tex. But the warning wasn't really necessary. All the cats were only too well aware that Basher was amongst them.

Some of them jumped up on to the fence, and there were so many cats on it that it began to sway about with the weight. Others dashed through the gate into the Rooneys' garden. More jumped and scrambled up into the tree. A number ran off down the lane, and from there leaped on to walls and up on to the roofs of houses to make their escape.

But Sheelagh was so angry she shouted: "You're just a great bully, Boris! Come on, cats, you know what they say about fighting like Cats and Dogs. Let's do just that!" She jumped at Boris and seized hold of his tail. The big brown cat said: "Down with Dogs!"

167

and grabbed one of Boris's back legs and pulled. Boris tripped and fell down.

Guinness and Butterscotch jumped on top of him. Wolf snapped and snarled at him. The big dog struggled to his feet, and began running round in circles, barking and lunging at every cat in his path.

Wolf said to Tex and Sheelagh: "I've got an idea. Quick, come into my garden. Look at this." The cats noticed the tap on the back of the shed. There was a green hose attached to it.

"Grab the end of that," said Wolf, "and point it from the roof of the shed down into the lane. If I get hold of the tap, I think I can turn it on."

Tex and Sheelagh got the nozzle of the hose in their mouths, and ran up on to the shed. They pointed it towards Boris, who was still rushing around and terrorising the few cats that were left. They saw Wolf with his mouth on the tap, trying to turn it. Soon the water began to flow. Tex and Sheelagh pointed the nozzle, and the jet of water hit Boris.

He gave a yelp of rage, and backed away, trying to avoid the water. But Tex and Sheelagh kept the hose pointed at him. Whenever he opened his jaws to bark, he got a mouthful of water.

"What on earth is going on?" It was Dick's voice. He came out into the lane, followed by a group of the children. They gazed at the scene in amazement. Just then, Boris decided he had had enough. He turned and ran off down the lane, with his wet tail between his legs.

"Victory! Victory!" yelled Tex. "Well done, Wolf!"

"Well done, Tex and Sheelagh!" said Wolf proudly.

"What a great end to the show!" said Guinness.

Sheelagh nudged Tex. "Look at the children," she said. "Just as we thought—Seamus is missing."

"He must be still upstairs," said Tex. "Come on!"

The two kittens jumped down from the shed into the lane, dashed past Dick and the children through the gate, and ran into the house. They hurried up the stairs and looked into the work-room.

There was Seamus, sitting in Dick's chair at the desk, gazing at the screen of the word processor. He had a notebook in one hand, and a pencil in the other, and was busily copying things from the screen.

"We've got him!" said Tex. Hearing the miaow, Seamus looked round. Then he chuckled.

"Oh, it's only you!" he said. "Just as well you can't talk, isn't it? I'm sure you'd give me away." He went on writing in his notebook.

"We'll give you away, all right!" said Sheelagh. "Come on, Tex!" The two kittens jumped on to the desk. Tex began to run up and down on the keyboard, hissing at Seamus.

Seamus said: "Here, watch it! The script's all gone

into a load of nonsense." As he got hold of Tex in both hands to move him away, Sheelagh grabbed the notebook and jumped down on to the floor.

"Give that back!" cried Seamus, but he was too late. Sheelagh was rushing down the stairs, just as Dick and the other children came in from the garden. Tex followed her down. Seamus came clattering down after them.

Sheelagh jumped on to a table, with the notebook in her mouth. She began waving it about from side to side. Tex jumped up beside her, and started yelling: "Stop Thief! Stop Thief!" at Seamus, as he tried to snatch the notebook from Sheelagh.

"What's that you've got there, Sheelagh?" asked Dick.

"It's mine, it's mine!" said Seamus.

"Let's have a look," said Dick. He took the notebook from Sheelagh. Seamus reached out and tried to snatch it out of Dick's hand.

"What's up, Seamus?" said Dick. "Why don't you want me to see it?"

"It's private," said Seamus, miserably, as Dick looked down at the open notebook. As he read the words in it, his face grew angry.

"Private, is it?" he said. "You're right, it *is* private— it's my script! You were copying it down from the screen, weren't you? So *you* were the Joke Thief, all the time!"

Seamus could think of nothing to say. He just looked down, and gave a grunt. Dick went on: "What a piece of luck that Sheelagh happened to pick up your notebook!"

"Luck?" snorted Sheelagh.

"Good detective work, he means!" grinned Tex.

The door-bell rang. "That will be Mrs Hogan," said Dick. Seamus went pale.

"Don't tell her! Please don't tell her!" he pleaded.

"What do the rest of you think?" Dick asked. The others began arguing about it. Some were in favour of telling the teacher, others against. But they all thought Seamus deserved some kind of punishment for stealing the jokes.

The door-bell rang again. "Right, Seamus—go and let Mrs Hogan in, and I'll tell you what we'll do."

When Mrs Hogan came in, Dick told her that the school newspaper would be ready soon. He only had to finish printing everything out, and next time they could paste it all together, ready for making copies. "I'm going to add an item, too," said Dick, "about Seamus."

Seamus gasped and went paler than ever. Mrs Hogan looked at Dick questioningly. Dick said: "Seamus is going to do a lot of fund-raising. He's going to think up lots of ideas to get money for the Cat

Shelter. That's where we got Tex and Sheelagh from."

Seamus sighed with relief. "Yes, yes," he said eagerly. "I'll raise lots of money for the Shelter. Lots and lots."

"I'm glad to hear it," said Mrs Hogan. She looked at the notebook in Dick's hand. "Are those your notes for the newspaper?" she asked.

"No, no," said Dick. "It's just an old notebook the cats were playing with—isn't that right, Seamus?"

"Yes…yes, that's right," said Seamus.

Dick threw the notebook into the air, and Sheelagh jumped up and caught it. She flung it across to Tex, who grabbed it in his teeth and shook it. The children all laughed. Even Seamus managed a weak smile.

"CAT WATCH to the rescue!" said Sheelagh. Then she said: "Tex, if it hadn't been for us, what would the Joke Thief have committed?"

"I don't know," said Tex.

"The *PURR*-fect Crime!" said Sheelagh. They both laughed loudly, and then began to play a tug-of-war game—with the Joke Thief's notebook!

# THE CASE OF THE
# KIDNAPPED CAT!

# 1

## Fun and Games

"Breakfast! Breakfast!" called Moira, and in two seconds the kittens Tex and Sheelagh were beside her. She put down the cat-food in the bowl labelled CAT. Tex always said it had to be labelled because people were not very bright, and might eat out of it by mistake.

People were not able to eat quickly and neatly like cats. They had to have lots of plates and bits of metal with scoops and prongs which they called spoons and forks. And they took so long about their meals! Tex and Sheelagh got bored watching them.

So when their own breakfast was finished, the kittens went out through the cat-flap in the back door and into the garden. Then they slipped through one of the gaps in the iron gate, and into the lane that ran along behind the houses.

They looked around for their friends Guinness and Butterscotch, the cats next door.

"There's no sign of them yet," said Sheelagh. "They're probably still asleep." The kittens thought their friends were a bit lazy.

"Wait – listen!" said Tex. They pricked up their ears. From somewhere above them came a sound like a loud, slow, rhythmical purr. It was Butterscotch snoring, as she lay on the top of the shed just over the garden fence of the house at the back. It was on the flat roof of this shed that Tex and Sheelagh and their two friends had performed their song-and-dance show, the CAT WATCH FOLLIES, for an audience of more than fifty cats from the neighbourhood.

Wolf, the dog from the house at the back, had been in the show too, trotting up and down like a pony, with the kittens on his back.

"Let's play a trick on Butterscotch," Sheelagh whispered.

She jumped up on to the fence, and Tex followed. They crept along on to the roof of the shed, just beside the sleeping figure.

The kittens went close to her ear, and shouted: "WOOF! WOOF!" Butterscotch woke up with a

start and cried: "What? What?!" and rolled off the shed. She fell into the garden, just as Wolf the dog came out of his house. He ran up to Butterscotch, wagging his tail with pleasure.

But Butterscotch was not at all pleased. "Why did you do that?" she grumbled. "I was trying to sleep."

"Do what?" Wolf was bewildered.

"Give that loud bark," said Butterscotch.

"But I didn't . . ." Wolf began. Then he heard laughter from the top of the shed. He looked up and saw the kittens. Butterscotch saw them too.

"Very funny," said Butterscotch, sourly. She jumped up on to the shed and lay down again. Guinness came out of his house to see what was going on.

When he heard what had happened, he said: "Anyone who can wake up Butterscotch deserves a medal!"

Just then, Tex and Sheelagh heard the back door of their own house open, and the voice of Moira saying: "Well, I think you deserve a medal!"

The cats all looked round in surprise. Had Moira suddenly learned to understand what cats were saying? Usually, people only heard cat speech as miaows and purrs, though cats could understand what people said, perfectly well. If Moira had become the first human to understand cats, this was a big step forward. She could become a Cat Translator, and tell all the other people exactly what cats wanted. Soon cats would be in their rightful place, ruling the world – and what a wonderful, calm, peaceful world it would be!

But soon the kittens realised that Moira wasn't talking to *them* at all. She was speaking to her husband Dick, who was in the garden in a green track-suit, running on the spot.

"Thanks, Moira," he said. "An Olympic Gold Medal would look good on the wall."

"Knowing you," said Moira, "I expect you'd give it to the cats to play with."

"Good idea," said Tex.

"Off you go then," said Moira, "and don't jog too hard."

"Don't worry, I won't overdo it," Dick said. "But I'm sure the exercise is doing me good."

"I'm sure it is," said Moira. "I'm going out now, but I'll see you this afternoon."

Dick opened the gate, waved her goodbye, and ran off down the lane. Moira went indoors.

"What's he doing?" asked Guinness.

"They call it jogging," said Sheelagh. "I heard them talking about it the other night. It just means running around for a while, and it's supposed to make him more healthy."

"It sounds too energetic for *me*," said Butterscotch.

"We don't need to do any special running to stay healthy," said Tex. "People have to do all sorts of silly things – they just aren't as clever as cats, you see."

"We could beat them at running if we wanted to," said Sheelagh.

"And at most other things too," said Tex. "We could win *all* the Olympic medals."

"What are they?" Guinness asked.

Tex and Sheelagh had heard all about the Olympic Games when Dick and Moira were watching a television programme about them. The kittens told their friends about the games and races and the Gold, Silver and Bronze medals which were awarded to the winners.

"It must be exhausting," said Butterscotch.

"You'd win the Gold Medal for Longest Sleeper," said Guinness.

"And I'd win it for Fastest Tail Wagger!" said Wolf.

"And Tex for Most Gobbling Eater!" Sheelagh laughed. But Tex didn't rise to this. He was thinking. Suddenly he said:

"Why shouldn't we do it too?"

"Do what?" The others were puzzled.

"Hold an Olympic Games – for cats!"

Sheelagh and Guinness thought it was a marvellous idea, and soon even Butterscotch got interested. She rather fancied herself with a Gold Medal or two draped around her neck.

They began to talk about what kind of events they would have. Then they noticed Wolf. He was sitting down, and looking very sad.

"What's the matter, Wolf?" asked Sheelagh.

"Nothing, really," said Wolf. "It's just that . . . if it's a Cat Olympics, I wouldn't be able to be in it. I'm a dog, you see," he explained rather unnecessarily.

"Cheer up, Wolf," said Sheelagh. "We'll have a special extra event for dogs *and* cats."

Wolf grinned happily. He had had such a good time since he got to know the cats. They were full of great ideas, like the CAT WATCH GANG, which they called themselves after Tex and Sheelagh helped to catch two burglars. Now it looked as if those skills might be needed again, for Tex suddenly said in a loud whisper: "Cat Watch Alert!" They all froze where they were.

"What's up?" whispered Sheelagh.

"Look!" said Tex. "Someone's coming up the lane, and I think he's up to no good."

# 2

## The Ladder Man

The cats stayed quite still and watched, as a young red-haired man in jeans and an anorak came up the lane. He was carrying a ladder on his shoulder. In the other hand he held a bucket.

"He's dressed just like one of those burglars who got into the house that night," whispered Sheelagh.

"We must warn Moira," said Tex.

"She said she was going out," Sheelagh said, "and Dick has gone off jogging."

"What's going on?" asked Wolf from behind the fence in his own garden.

"Ssssh!" said Tex. He jumped down and explained to Wolf about the man they thought was a burglar. "You can be our reserve force, Wolf," he said. "When we're ready, we'll open the latch of your gate and you can come out barking like mad."

Wolf nodded eagerly. Tex climbed back on to the shed.

The man had opened the gate into Dick and Moira's garden and gone in. He leaned the ladder up against the wall of the house, took the bucket and climbed up. He began rubbing at the window.

"That's the window to the room where Dick and Moira work," said Sheelagh. "Perhaps he wants to steal their computers."

"Yes, he'll put them in the bucket and take them away." Tex could always find a confident explanation.

"Why is he rubbing at the window?" asked Guinness.

"He must be trying to push it in," said Tex. "We've got to stop him. I'll go indoors through the cat-flap and upstairs. Then I can hiss at him through the window. He'll be scared off when he sees there's a Guard Cat inside." He jumped down off the shed and ran into the garden and through the cat-flap in the door. He bounded up the stairs and climbed on to a bookshelf just below the window.

Tex pressed his face against the window and glared and hissed at the man on the ladder. But to his dismay, the man didn't seem at all frightened. In fact, he smiled and waved at Tex through the window.

Tex snarled: "We know what you're up to! Cat Watch to the rescue! Get out of here!" He stood on his hind legs and beat at the glass with his front paws.

But of course the man only heard faint mews and hisses coming through the window. He said: "Do you want to get out, Puss? I can't help you, I'm afraid."

Tex disliked being called Puss, and renewed his battering at the glass, and his cries of: "Get out of here! Go away!"

Then he saw the man begin to climb down the ladder. Tex gave a grin of triumph. He jumped off the shelf, scampered down the stairs and dashed out of the cat-flap, nearly colliding with the feet of the man, who had just stepped off the bottom of the ladder.

"Watch out, Puss!" said the man.

Tex joined his friends on the roof of the shed. "See that!" he cried. "He's leaving! I scared him off."

The others congratulated him. "You're a great Guard Cat, Tex!" said Sheelagh. Suddenly Guinness said: "Wait a minute. Look at the man now. He doesn't seem to be leaving at all."

They all gazed back at the house. Indeed, the man was not leaving. In fact he had simply moved the ladder along a bit, and was climbing up it again. Soon he was rubbing and pushing at another window. While he did so, he whistled a tune.

"He doesn't look very frightened," said Butterscotch.

"He's just trying another window," said Tex. "We'll have to fall back on Battle Plan B."

"What's that?" asked Guinness.

In fact, Tex had no Battle Plan B, he just thought it sounded good. But he was a quick thinker. "Full Force Attack!" he said.

"We'll open Wolf's gate, and he can bark at

186

the back gate of our house, through the gaps. We'll all go through ourselves and climb up the ladder and tackle the burglar."

Sheelagh ran along the fence, put her paw down and pushed open the latch of the gate to Wolf's garden. The dog butted the gate with his head, and it swung open. He went into the lane. The cats jumped down beside him.

"Everyone ready?" asked Tex.

"Ready!" said Sheelagh.

"Ready!" said Guinness.

"Woof!" said Wolf.

Butterscotch yawned. Tex glared at her, and she said with a sigh: "Ready."

"Right," Tex said. "One, two, three – ATTACK!"

Wolf went to the gate and began barking fiercely. The cats ran through the gaps in the gate which were too narrow for Wolf. They scrambled up the sides and rungs of the ladder, and grabbed the man's jeans with their teeth. "Here!" he cried, looking down. "What are you doing, you silly moggies?"

He stuck out his left leg and shook it about. Guinness lost his grip and fell to the ground. Tex hung on, but then the man's bucket tilted and a great splosh of water drenched Tex. He let go and fell down beside Guinness.

"Are you OK?" asked Guinness.

"Fine, don't worry," said Tex. Just then the man dropped the bucket and the rest of the water splashed out on top of Guinness and Tex, while the bucket itself crashed down just beside them.

Sheelagh and Butterscotch were still hanging on to the man's other leg. He began to shake that one, but still the cats clung on.

Down below, Tex and Guinness gave shouts of encouragement, and Wolf barked even more loudly.

Then as the man stretched his leg further backwards, the cats saw the top of the ladder come away from the wall. Now the man was balancing on it as it stood upright, swaying from side to side in the air.

"What's going on?" It was the voice of Dick, who had come jogging back up the lane and now saw the noisy happenings in the garden. He opened the gate and went in, just as the ladder toppled and fell down, scattering Sheelagh and Butterscotch, and nearly crashing down on Tex and Guinness.

The man fell on top of Dick, and both of them sprawled on the ground. They sat up, and looked around. The four cats sat in a group, staring at them. Wolf stopped barking and sat down.

"What happened?" asked Dick.

"Those moggies came up the ladder after me!" said the man. "I don't know what they've got against me – I like cats. Most cats, anyway. But that lot are wild – and dangerous!"

Tex and Sheelagh smiled at one another with pride.

"The kittens are ours, Paddy," said Dick. "We got them since you last cleaned our windows. They wouldn't hurt anyone."

"Not much!" Paddy grumbled. "Look at my jeans – they're torn to bits."

"What were you doing?" Dick asked.

"What do you think I was doing? I was up the ladder with my bucket . . ."

Suddenly Dick started to laugh.

"It's not funny," Paddy said.

"I'm sorry," said Dick. "It's just that I've realised what must have happened. The cats thought you were a burglar."

Tex and Sheelagh looked at each other again, but this time they weren't smiling. "He's *not* a burglar!" said Sheelagh.

"Then what is he?" asked Tex suspiciously. They soon discovered.

"Well, I tell you one thing," said the man, getting up and dusting himself down. "That's the last time I clean your windows! A bloke would need Danger Money for this job."

"I hope you'll change your mind, Paddy,"

said Dick. "The cats thought you were another burglar. They're very clever creatures."

"Clever they may be, but you'd need to tame them before I'd risk another visit," said Paddy.

Dick realised it was no use protesting just now. He fished a note out of his track-suit pocket, and gave it to Paddy, who picked up his ladder and his bucket, gave a final glare at the cats, and went out of the gate and down the lane.

Dick waited till he was out of sight. He looked at the cats. Tex and Sheelagh wondered if he was going to tell them off. But they relaxed when suddenly he burst out laughing.

# 3

## Fifi Comes to Stay

"Well, I think Tex and Sheelagh were very brave," said Moira, when Dick told her about the attack on the ladder man.

"I agree," said Tex. The kittens were sitting under the table, while Dick and Moira had their evening meal. They could never understand why they weren't allowed to get on to the table and share the meal. It seemed unfair. After all, Tex and Sheelagh would not have minded if Dick and Moira decided to kneel down and eat with *them* out of the bowl marked CAT.

"Yes, they *were* brave," said Dick. "They just didn't understand."

"I hope they'll understand about Fifi," said Moira.

Tex and Sheelagh looked at each other, puzzled. Who was Fifi? they wondered.

"Oh, Fifi won't be any trouble, I'm sure," said Dick. "Patsy says she's a lovely cat."

"What else would your sister say? It's *her* cat. And she's as soppy about Fifi as we are about ours."

"Well, they'll only be here for a few days – until the Cat Show. Fifi might win a prize. She's a really high-class cat, Patsy says. One of the best of her breed."

Sheelagh and Tex didn't like the sound of Fifi at all. It was bad enough having a strange cat coming to stay with them, but one that was so "high-class" might think it was too grand for them. After all, they were described on their vet's certificate only as BREED: DOMESTIC.

"What did you say her breed was?" asked Moira.

"Persian of some kind. White Longhair, I think it's called."

"It sounds as if Fifi needs a hair-cut!" said Sheelagh.

And when she arrived next day, Fifi certainly did live up to her breed's name of Longhair.

She climbed slowly out of the cat-basket which Patsy had put on the living-room floor.

Dick and Moira stood looking at her, smiling, as Patsy patted her head and said: "Come along, Fifi! Come and meet your new friends."

The new friends were not looking very friendly. Tex and Sheelagh were each curled up in their favourite chair and sofa, pretending to be asleep. But they each had one eye a bit open, to see the new arrival.

Fifi stood in the middle of the floor, and looked around her. She had a coat of long, white, fluffy fur that stuck out all over her. It looked soft and fine. Her eyes were a bright orange colour.

"Welcome, Fifi!" said Moira. She smiled at Tex and Sheelagh, who said nothing and didn't move.

Fifi gazed around the room, as if she was deciding whether it was good enough for her to stay in. She must have seen Tex and Sheelagh, but she pretended to ignore them.

Then she walked slowly across to the rug in

front of the fireplace, stretched, curled up and went to sleep.

"She seems to have made herself at home," said Patsy, laughing a little nervously.

Tex glared sourly at Fifi. The rug in front of the fireplace was one of his favourite spots.

"Come through and have some tea, Patsy," said Moira. "Then we'll show you your room."

The three cats were left alone in the living-room. Tex and Sheelagh both sat up, and looked at each other. Then at the same moment they jumped down and walked across to the rug. They stood one each side of the sleeping Fifi.

195

"Howdy!" said Tex, in an accent like he'd heard from the television box when Dick and Moira were watching what they called a cowboy film.

"Hi there, pardner!" said Sheelagh, in the same style.

Fifi opened her eyes and rolled them around to gaze at the two cats in turn. Then she sat up.

"How do you do?" she said. Her voice was high and sharp. "My name is Fifi."

Tex decided to try being polite. "I'm Tex," he said. "And this is Sheelagh."

"We live here," Sheelagh said.

"Really?" said Fifi, looking round the room as if she was surprised.

Then she stared at the two kittens and said loftily: "I am a White Longhair Persian. What breed are you?"

"Domestic – First Class," said Sheelagh.

"Never heard of it," said Fifi. "Are you going to enter for the Cat Show too?"

"We haven't made up our minds," said Tex. "We might, if we can spare the time."

Fifi stared at Tex and Sheelagh. They stared back. It became a challenge. Who would look away first? The three cats stood like statues for a minute or more. Finally Sheelagh got bored. She said: "Well, we're off to do a bit of practice for the Games. Are you coming, Fifi?"

"Yes, come along," said Tex. "You can show us what you're good at."

Fifi looked puzzled. "Good at?" she said.

"Yes," said Sheelagh. "You know: high jump, long jump, somersaults, whisker-twitching, fast rolling-over, paw-ball . . ."

"I don't play any games," said Fifi, with her head in the air. "They're too rough, you see. I might get scratched, or my fur might get dirty."

"Oh, we wouldn't want that!" said Sheelagh. "What about boxing, then?"

She was just raising her paw menacingly, when Moira and Patsy came in.

"Come along, Fifi," said Patsy, "Moira will show us where we're going to sleep." She picked up the fluffy cat and went on: "You can play with your new friends later."

"Any time!" said Tex.

Fifi gave a miaow that sounded very like a sneer.

Outside in the lane, Tex and Sheelagh let off some of their annoyance with some energetic high-jumping on to the fence, and some hectic tail-chasing. Chasing your own tail round and round in circles was fun, but it made you a bit dizzy. The two kittens were sitting down, feeling as if their heads were whirling, when Guinness and Butterscotch appeared.

"Go on, Guinness," said Tex, "let's see you chase your tail!"

"I am too dignified a cat to do silly things like that," said Guinness.

The others smiled. They knew that Guinness was really too fat for such an energetic sport.

"If you think *you're* dignified, you should see who's come to stay at our house," said Sheelagh.

They told their friends all about Fifi and her snooty ways.

"She's got a cheek, turning up her nose at us," said Sheelagh, "just because her breed has got some fancy name."

"Bring her out to us," said Guinness, pushing

out his shoulders in his tough-guy stance. "We'll sort her out."

"No, that wouldn't be fair," said Tex. "Four against one."

"I offered to give her a boxing match," said Sheelagh.

"She wouldn't fight," said Tex. "She'd be afraid to ruffle her fur."

"We must think of some other way of bringing her down a bit," said Sheelagh.

And as it happened, that evening they heard of what looked like the perfect opportunity.

Moira and Dick and Patsy were sitting in the living-room, talking, after the evening meal. Tex had plonked himself down on the fireplace rug, just to show it was his territory. Sheelagh was on the sofa, beside Moira.

Fifi was sitting on the floor at the feet of Patsy, who was stroking her head.

Dick said: "Patsy, we've got a friend called Liam, who's a photographer. He's trying to get together some photographs for the papers to publish in the days coming up to the Cat Show.

I told him you'd be here with Fifi, and I was sure you wouldn't mind if he came and took a picture."

"I'd be delighted," said Patsy. "And so would Fifi, I'm sure!"

Sheelagh and Tex both glanced at Fifi through hooded eyes. The fluffy white cat looked up at Patsy with a sickly smile, and twitched her whiskers, as if to say: "If it's beautiful photographs you want, I'm your cat!"

Then Sheelagh and Tex looked at one another. The same thought was in both their minds: they'd make sure the photograph session didn't work out the way Fifi hoped.

# 4

## Unhappy Snaps

Next morning, Tex and Sheelagh were puzzled as they watched Dick and Moira spread an old rug on top of the living-room carpet.

"Perhaps it's for some kind of a game," said Sheelagh.

"We could use it to play a game ourselves," said Tex with a smile. "We'll call it ROLLING FIFI UP IN A RUG!"

They both laughed and began scampering about, pulling at the rug.

"You can play with it later, kittens," said Moira, straightening it. "At the moment, we need it for Fifi."

"Surely *they're* not going to roll her up in it?" Tex wondered.

Then they watched as Patsy brought Fifi out of her room, and put her carefully down on the rug. Then she knelt down beside her, and produced a large brush. She began brushing the long white fur of the cat, who sat with her eyes closed, delighted with herself, as if this kind of attention was simply what she deserved.

"We must look our best in the photograph, mustn't we, Fifi?" said Patsy.

Fifi smiled her superior smile.

Moira came over and stroked Tex and Sheelagh, so that they wouldn't feel left out.

"I wonder why they don't brush us like that," Sheelagh said.

"We don't need brushing," said Tex loftily. "We keep our own fur smooth and glossy, by licking it. Those long-haired cats are useless when it comes to looking after themselves."

Dick was out jogging, and Moira soon went into the kitchen, leaving Tex and Sheelagh to watch the hairdressing job being done on Fifi.

"This is more boring than watching people looking at the television," said Sheelagh. "Let's go out and do some Games practice."

They went out through the cat-flap and then

through the garden to the lane. As usual, Butterscotch was asleep on top of the fence. Guinness was sitting on the roof of the nearby shed, washing himself.

"You see," said Tex, "Guinness can clean himself like we can. It's only silly cats like Fifi who have to be brushed and pampered."

Guinness looked up, and Tex and Sheelagh told him about the brushing session going on inside.

"Fifi is having her photograph taken," said Sheelagh.

"And we're going to make sure we're in it, too," said Tex.

"I don't suppose Fifi will like that," Guinness said.

"That's the whole idea!" said Sheelagh.

"Never mind Fifi," said Tex, keen to be busy. "Let's do some Games practice. How about a spell of hind-legs fence-walking?"

He jumped up on to the fence, stood on his hind-legs with his front paws in the air, and began tiptoeing along the fence. When he came to Butterscotch, he pretended not to see her, and trod on her tail.

Butterscotch woke with a screech, and sat up, knocking Tex off balance.

Tex jumped down off the fence, and Butterscotch wobbled, lost her own balance, and fell into the lane, just managing to land on her feet.

"What did you do that for?" Butterscotch grumbled.

Tex smiled innocently: "Sorry, I didn't see you. We Olympic high-steppers don't expect cats to be sleeping in our path."

Just then, Dick came jogging up the lane, back from his run. He seemed very out of breath, and was panting a lot.

"He says the exercise does him good," said Tex, as Dick stopped thankfully at the gate.

"I'd rather not risk it," said Butterscotch, yawning.

Moira came out into the courtyard and saw Dick in the lane. She opened the gate and came out.

"Liam just phoned," she said. "He'll be here in about half an hour."

"Good, I'll have time to shower and get changed," said Dick.

Moira smiled: "Anyone would think it was you being photographed."

"My hair isn't quite as long as Fifi's," Dick said, stroking his balding head, "and talking of fine hair, you know the place I told you about, that I pass on my run: WALSH'S CATTERY?"

"Yes, you mentioned it," said Moira.

"Well, today I met the woman who owns it – Julia Walsh. She told me that as well as running a boarding-house for cats, she breeds Persians. I told her we had one staying with us, and she said she would love to see it. So I said she could drop in some time."

"Is she putting any of her cats in the Cat Show?"

"Yes, one – a real champion, she says. It's called the Duchess of Dingle, would you believe! And it's won several prizes."

Dick and Moira went inside.

"The more I hear about these Persian cats," said Tex, "the more I dislike them. Champions, prizes! They must be a stuck-up lot."

"We'll have our own champions and prizes," said Sheelagh, "now that we're holding the Cat Olympics."

"Come on," said Tex, "let's do some more

fence-walking!" He jumped on to the fence, followed by Sheelagh. They both stood up on their hind-legs and began stepping delicately along the fence. Guinness jumped up and followed. His weight made him wobble about a bit, but he just managed to keep his footing. Finally Butterscotch climbed up behind him, and joined in the strange march along the fence. They looked like a line of ballet-dancers.

Suddenly they heard the sound of barking from below. Sheelagh looked down and saw Wolf. "Hi, Wolf!" she said. "How do you like our neat footwork?"

"Terrific," said Wolf. "Now, watch me!"

Wolf stood up on his hind-legs, and began to stagger about on the grass, waving his front legs in the air. The cats on the fence stopped walking, and sat down to watch him. Wolf kept it up for more than half a minute, then fell over. The cats all cheered.

"Well done, Wolf," said Tex. "You'll definitely win the gold medal for Hind-Legs Walking."

Just then they heard voices in their own garden. Dick and Moira had come out of the house with Patsy, who was carrying Fifi in her

arms. With them was a man with untidy fair hair, wearing a leather jacket. He had a camera hanging on a cord round his neck.

"It's only a small garden, Liam," Dick said, "but it might make a good enough background."

"It will do fine," Liam said. "Suppose we tried sitting Fifi on that garden chair, in front of the rose-bush there."

Sitting on the fence outside, the four cats could see across the lane and in through the wrought-iron gate. Patsy put Fifi on the garden chair. The cat put her head in the air and looked from side to side, as if she was trying out whether the left or right side of her face would look better in the picture.

"That's good," said Liam. He raised the camera to his eye.

The cats on the fence looked at one another.

"What a ridiculous fuss," said Tex. "We'd look much better in a picture than that white fluff-ball."

"What's going on?" asked Wolf. He could see nothing from his garden on the other side of the fence.

Sheelagh had an idea: "We'll let you out, Wolf, and you can have a look." She winked at her friends. She had a good idea that the sight of Wolf might make Fifi a lot less smug and pleased with herself.

Sheelagh ran along the fence and leaned over and pushed down the latch, so that Wolf could nose the gate open. The dog came bustling into the lane, his tail wagging.

"Over there, Wolf," said Sheelagh, pointing at the gate. "See that white cloud of fur? That's a cat, believe it or not."

"Really?" said Wolf. He went across to the gate and peered through a gap in the ironwork. Liam was just raising his camera to take another shot.

"Woof!" said Wolf.

Fifi looked over at the gate and saw the grinning face of Wolf gazing at her. She gave a shriek of fright, and jumped into the air. When she came down she began rushing around the small garden looking for somewhere to hide.

"He's after me, he's after me! Get him away!" she cried.

Wolf gave another bark which he meant to be friendly. But Fifi shrieked even louder, and hid behind a bush, shivering.

On the fence, Tex and Sheelagh and their friends were chuckling happily.

"It's no good trying to photograph her like that," said Liam. "We'd better bring her inside."

Patsy picked Fifi up and glared at Wolf. Even though Dick and Moira told her Wolf wouldn't do any harm and got on fine with their cats, Patsy just grunted and took the white cat indoors. The rest of them followed.

"Well done, Wolf," said Tex. "Round One to us!"

"Now let's go inside, for Round Two," said Sheelagh.

# 5

# Chasing the Star

Tex and Sheelagh slipped through a gap in the iron gate and went across the garden and into the house through the cat flap. Just inside the door, they saw Liam kneeling down and rummaging in the case which contained his camera gear. Dick was standing beside him. Moira and Patsy had gone through into the living-room with Fifi.

"I'll have to use an extra spotlight for this one," said Liam. "Could you hand me that metal stand over there?"

Dick picked up a long metal rod from the floor, with a tripod on the end, and stood it up. Liam began fixing a light to it. He looked worried.

"I want to get these pictures right," he said. "It's a good chance for me, and there hasn't been much work around."

"Yes, it's tough without a regular job," said Dick. "The writing game is the same. You have to take what you can get."

Tex and Sheelagh wandered on into the living-room. Tex glared when he saw Fifi sitting on the fireplace rug. Patsy was kneeling beside her, patting her down.

"There, there, Fifi," she said. "You're safe from the big bad dog now."

The idea of anyone being afraid of Wolf made Sheelagh smile.

He was just about the soppiest dog you could ever imagine, and he and the four cats had become great friends.

Liam came in with the lamp-stand and saw Fifi on the rug.

"That's a good place," he said. "Can we light the fire?"

"It's a bit warm for that, isn't it?" said Moira. "But still, for the sake of the picture . . ." She bent down and turned on the gas-tap which lit up the flames behind the fake coals in the fireplace.

"Great," said Liam, putting the spotlight in position and plugging it in. He flicked the switch, and a bright light shone on Fifi and the rug. Fifi blinked her orange eyes, then stood up and wriggled in a swaggering kind of way before she sat down again, smiling, with her head raised high. She just loved being the centre of attraction.

"Perfect," said Liam. "Now if she can hold it, just like that, it will be grand."

Sheelagh and Tex were sitting just beside the spotlight stand.

They looked at one another. Tex grinned, and then jumped up and clutched hold of the stand, holding on with all four paws round it.

The stand swayed from side to side.

"Watch out!" cried Liam. The stand rocked like a palm tree in a high wind, and just as it was about to topple over, Tex jumped clear. Liam just managed to catch hold of the stand before it crashed to the floor. He fell down, holding it up to save the bulb from breaking.

Tex and Sheelagh sat looking on innocently, as Dick helped Liam up.

"That cat is a menace," said Liam.

"He just wanted to play," said Moira.

Tex smiled sweetly. He looked across and saw Fifi staring at him with anger in her eyes. She knew that Tex wasn't playing at all.

The spotlight was set up again, Fifi posed as before, and Liam lined up his camera. "That's good," he said.

This time Sheelagh decided to get into the act. She rushed forward, right in front of Fifi, flung herself on to the floor, and began rolling about on her back, with her legs in the air.

Fifi bared her teeth with rage, just as the camera clicked.

"That's hopeless!" said Liam.

"Ah, look at Sheelagh," said Moira. "She wants her tummy rubbed." She went over and tickled Sheelagh's fur.

"Never mind her tummy!" snapped Liam, "what about my picture?"

"There's no need to shout," said Moira.

"I'm sorry," said Liam. "But I'll never get this shot if those cats of yours keep messing things up. Couldn't you shut them away somewhere?"

"Well, it *is* their house, after all," said Dick.

Sheelagh sat up, pleased, and she and Tex

began rubbing themselves up against Dick and Moira's legs.

"All right, let's try again," Liam sighed.

Once more, he lined up the camera, while Patsy stroked Fifi to try to calm her down.

Just as Fifi struck her pose again, Tex called out: "Fifi, there's a wasp on your left ear."

"What?!" shrieked Fifi, scratching frantically at her ear with her back paw.

"Now it's jumped on to your tail!" said Tex.

Fifi shrieked again, and began turning round and round, snapping at her own tail. Patsy was trying to calm her, and Liam was standing with his hand to his head, glaring furiously.

Then Tex smiled and said to Fifi: "It's OK, Fifi – I was only joking!"

The fluffy cat stopped her whirling and stood very still, staring hard at Tex, who stared back, grinning.

Suddenly Fifi gave a yelp of rage, bared her teeth and rushed at Tex. But he was too quick for her. He leaped backwards away from her, then turned round and dashed to the back door and through the cat-flap into the garden. Fifi ran after him, and Sheelagh followed.

Tex ran ahead through the iron gate into the lane. Then he turned to look back at his pursuer.

Fifi put her head through one of the gaps in the iron gate, and nearly got stuck. Sheelagh came up behind her and nipped at her tail. "Ouch!" cried Fifi, and pushed through. Then she stopped in her tracks.

Standing in front of her, like a line of footballers protecting a goal, were Tex, Guinness and Butterscotch – and the large bulk of Wolf. Sheelagh dashed past Fifi and joined the end of the line.

"Hi there, Fifi!" said Guinness, in his most menacing voice. "Have you come to train for the Cat Olympics?"

Fifi knew better than to start any kind of a fight, when this lot were ranged against her.

"Certainly not," she said. "I only compete in Cat Shows."

"What as?" asked Butterscotch.

"A Persian Longhair, of course."

"Well, I'm a Kerry Red Hair," said Butterscotch. She turned towards Guinness and said: "And he's a Guinness Stout Hair."

Sheelagh was enjoying this. She pointed to Wolf and said:

"Do you know what he is? He's a Labrador Floppy Ear!"

Wolf gave a barking laugh. Fifi shrank back. She didn't know dogs could ever be friendly to cats. And anyway, right now, none of them *looked* very friendly.

She stood staring at the four cats and the dog. If she had made some gesture of friendship now, they would have welcomed her to the gang. But she didn't understand that. She didn't have any cat friends: she was used to being praised and stroked and petted by people. No wonder she thought she was a star.

So when Tex said: "Here, Fifi, can you do this?" and began walking on his hind-legs, she only turned up her nose and said:

"No – and I wouldn't want to."

Tex got down again. He glared at Fifi, then looked at the others. As if at a signal, they all began advancing on Fifi in a line, slowly, step by step. She began to back away, expecting at any moment that they would leap on her, sinking their teeth into her fluffy fur. But they just kept moving towards her, until her back was to the iron gate.

In panic, Fifi turned and pushed through a gap. She ran across the garden, and nosed her way through the cat-flap into the house.

Outside, the Cat Watch Gang were laughing to themselves.

Sheelagh said to the others: "See you later! It's time for another photograph session!" She and Tex followed Fifi into the house.

Patsy was patting her. She picked her up and put her back on the fireplace rug.

Liam said wearily: "OK, let's give it another try."

Just then the doorbell rang.

"Never a dull moment!" smiled Dick, as Liam raised his hands to his head in despair. He wondered if he would ever get his picture of Fifi.

Tex and Sheelagh followed Dick out into the hall. He opened the front door. A plump woman with curly brown hair stood on the doorstep. She was wearing an anorak and jeans.

"Hello there!" she said.

"Mrs Walsh!" said Dick.

"Please, call me Julia," said the visitor. "I hope you don't mind me taking up your invitation so soon, but I just couldn't wait to have a look at your house-guest, Fifi."

"It's a pleasure," Dick said. "She's in the living-room right now, having her photograph taken. Please come in."

Mrs Walsh stepped through the front door and saw Tex and Sheelagh. "And these must be your own two little moggies," she said. "How sweet!"

She went through into the living-room, leaving Tex and Sheelagh looking far from pleased.

# 6

# Champions

The two kittens followed Dick and Julia into the living-room.

Julia exclaimed: "Ah! This must be Fifi! Isn't she beautiful!"

She bent down and stroked Fifi behind her ear. The white Persian smiled happily. There was nothing she liked better than being admired.

Julia Walsh stood back and gazed at Fifi. "Would you stand her up for me?" she asked. "Then I can get a better idea of her good points."

Patsy set Fifi on her feet. Julia Walsh stared at her for a while, then knelt down and felt her body and her legs, and stroked her tail. She put her hand under Fifi's chin and stared into her face.

"What a fuss about a bundle of fur!" said Tex.

Sheelagh opened her mouth and gave a huge yawn.

Finally, Julia Walsh said: "I congratulate you. Fifi really is a wonderful specimen of the breed. And worth a fortune, of course."

"Really?" said Patsy. "I hadn't thought about that – we just keep her as a pet. Then I decided it might be fun to come and visit Dick and Moira, and put her in the Cat Show at the same time."

"I wouldn't be surprised if she walks off with the prize," said Julia.

"What about your own cat?" said Dick. "She's a champion, isn't she?"

"The Duchess of Dingle? Oh yes, she's one of the best," said Julia, "but Fifi will be stiff competition for her."

Tex and Sheelagh saw Fifi look across at them with a superior smile. Tex stuck out his tongue at her.

Liam said to Julia: "Perhaps I could come and photograph your cat for the series?"

"Any time, I'd be delighted," said Julia, handing him a white business card.

Patsy looked a little annoyed. So did Fifi.

"And in the meantime," said Liam, "we must get that photograph of Fifi."

Patsy put Fifi back in her pose on the rug. Liam adjusted his lighting again, then fiddled with his camera. "OK, I'm ready," he said.

Tex and Sheelagh looked at one another. Then they both got up and strolled across towards Fifi. They lay down on the rug, one each side of her.

"Oh no!" said Liam, "not again!"

"They just want to be in the picture too," said Moira fondly.

"Why not let them?" said Julia. "Fifi will look all the better beside the two moggies."

Fifi wasn't at all pleased to have Tex and Sheelagh sharing her spotlight, and the kittens certainly weren't pleased to be there to show how high-class Fifi was. So the more Fifi struck poses, trying to look superior, the more Tex and Sheelagh imitated her, sticking their heads in the air and looking down their noses.

Dick and Moira were delighted with their antics, though Patsy seemed to find it less entertaining. Liam took a number of shots, but he still seemed anxious to get a solo photograph of Fifi.

"Perhaps we could do it somewhere else," he said desperately, eyeing Tex and Sheelagh.

"You could go into your room if you like, Patsy," said Moira.

So Patsy carried Fifi across the hall to the spare bedroom which was at the front of the house. Liam followed, and so did Julia Walsh.

Tex reclaimed his rightful place on the fireplace rug, and Sheelagh curled up on her sofa.

She called across to Tex: "Here's a riddle, Tex. What do they call it when a Longhair Persian cat gets an Olympic prize by mistake?"

"I don't know," said Tex.

"An Olympic Gold Muddle!" They both laughed, and settled down to have a sleep.

At last, Liam packed up his gear and left. Julia Walsh went with him. She was going to take him to see her own champion cat, as well as the Cattery itself where she took cats in for boarding when their owners were going away.

Fifi stayed in Patsy's room. She wouldn't talk to Tex and Sheelagh, after they had tried to mess up her moment of stardom.

The two kittens went out into the lane to find Butterscotch and Guinness and tell them all about the photograph session. They were sitting on the fence, chatting away, when they saw a figure come up the lane. It was Paddy, the window-cleaner.

When he saw them, he looked at them with great distrust, and edged carefully past on the other side of the lane, as far away from them as he could get. He thought they might attack him again. They watched him open the garden gate, go through and knock at the back door. Dick came out.

The cats heard Paddy telling Dick he was sorry he went off in such a temper, but if it was all right, he would be pleased to come and clean the windows as he used to do.

Dick explained that now the cats knew who he was, they wouldn't cause any trouble. But there was another prize cat staying just now who might not understand. So he and Dick agreed that Paddy would come next week when the Cat Show was over.

As Paddy went off down the lane, Tex and Sheelagh called:

"See you soon, Paddy!" They meant to be

friendly, but Paddy only heard a miaowing sound and thought they were angry. He looked at them with alarm, and hurried away.

"People are really very stupid," said Tex. "They don't understand when we are being nice to them."

"He understood that we *weren't* being nice, last time!" said Guinness. They all laughed.

That night Dick and Moira went out with Patsy. Tex said to Fifi: "We're going to do some night Olympic Games practice. Do you want to come?"

"Certainly not," said Fifi.

"Suit yourself," said Sheelagh.

Fifi stalked off into the spare room. Tex and Sheelagh went out into the lane. They called Guinness and Butterscotch, who ran out of their own house to join them.

Wolf came out into his garden and saw them on the fence. He ambled over and asked what games they were going to practise. "You can't do much in the dark," he said.

"Oh yes, we can!" said Sheelagh. "Cats can see in the dark, didn't you know? I can see you very well, Wolf, but I bet you can't see me properly."

"I can," said Wolf, peering upwards.

"Cats' eyes are much better than dogs', it's a well-known fact," said Tex.

"Maybe, but our sense of smell is a lot better than yours," said Wolf. "That's why people use us for tracking, and sniffing things out."

"Cats could do that," said Guinness. "We just can't be bothered."

"All right," said Wolf. "Let's have a competition. A Sniffing-in-the-Dark Contest!"

They agreed that Sheelagh would go and hide somewhere in Wolf's garden, and they would all try and sniff out where she was.

"Shut your eyes, then," said Sheelagh, "and count to twenty, before you come looking for me."

She jumped down into Wolf's garden and looked around. There were lots of bushes and shrubs and trees where she could hide. She roamed around the garden, trying to decide. She could hear the booming voice of Guinness counting: ". . . nine . . . ten . . ."

She dashed across the garden, round the fish-pond in the middle, and back towards the fence. There was a tree there, with a small platform high up in it which had originally been meant to be a bird-table. The birds were too afraid to hang around much, now that so many cats were always in the lane.

As Guinness counted " . . . seventeen . . . eighteen . . . " Sheelagh reached the bottom of the tree. She scampered up it and lay crouched down on the flat bird-table, out of sight.

She heard Guinness say: " . . . nineteen . . . twenty! We're coming to find you, Sheelagh!"

Then she watched as the three cats jumped down into the garden. Tex went off towards Wolf's house, and Guinness stared around, then began looking along the bottom of the fence. Butterscotch set off across the garden, padding along lazily, looking up in the air as though she expected to see Sheelagh gliding above her.

She was so busy looking up that she nearly stepped straight into the pond. She jumped back just in time, and lay down on the grass to recover from the shock.

While the cats went their various ways, Wolf put his nose to the ground. Sheelagh watched him sniff away, very sure of himself, following exactly the track that she had taken across the grass and then back towards the tree. Soon he was down at the bottom of the tree, looking up at the platform.

"Found you, Sheelagh!" he barked excitedly.

Sheelagh sat up. "I've got to admit it, Wolf," she said. "You're the winner!"

After that, they took it in turns to hide. Wolf was always first to find them. When it was his own turn, he hid under a bush, but he was panting so loudly with all the rushing about, that they found him straight away.

The time seemed to pass very quickly. They saw lights go on in their house. Dick and Moira and Patsy must be back.

Then the back door opened and Patsy and Dick came out into the courtyard. They opened the gate into the lane and Patsy called out: "Fifi! Fifi! Where are you?"

"It's all right," said Dick, "she must be around somewhere."

"No," said Patsy with a sob, "she's gone! Fifi's disappeared!"

# 7

# Catnapped

Dick shone a torch around the lane. He saw the four cats sitting on the fence. "Tex and Sheelagh are there," said Dick, "with those cats from next door. I wish we could ask *them* if they've seen Fifi."

Tex and Sheelagh looked at each other. Even if they replied, Dick would only hear what they said as a miaow sound. Besides, there was nothing they could tell him. They had seen no sign of Fifi since she went off into the spare room in a sulk, hours ago.

"We'll have another look indoors," said Dick. "She might be asleep in a cupboard somewhere." Dick and Patsy went back into the house, and Tex and Sheelagh followed.

"I can't see her outside," Dick told Moira. "Any luck here?"

"No," said Moira, "I've looked upstairs, and all through the house."

"She's gone!" Patsy sobbed.

"Let's have another look in your room," Moira said. They all went into the spare room, including Tex and Sheelagh. Moira bent down and gave them each a stroke. She was really pleased that *they* hadn't disappeared as well.

Tex and Sheelagh went sniffing around, like Wolf had done in the garden. They looked under the bed, and in the cupboard, and under the chest of drawers. There was no sign of Fifi.

Then Sheelagh jumped up on to the window-sill. "Look at this!" she said to Tex. He jumped up beside her.

"The window's not shut," said Sheelagh. She nudged it with her nose, and it opened a little. Then she gave it a push with her paw, and it opened some more.

Dick noticed. "See that!" he said. "The window wasn't properly shut. Fifi must have got out that way."

"I'm sure I shut it firmly before I left," said Patsy.

"Well, it's open now," said Dick.

"But how could she have opened it?" asked Moira.

Sheelagh was standing on her hind-legs, with her face up to the latch that shut the window. There were some scratches around it, and the metal of the latch looked a bit bent. She tapped at it with her paws to attract attention.

Dick came across and saw the scratches and the bent handle. "Look at this!" he said. "It seems to me that someone's been tampering with the handle. It could have been a screwdriver or something, pushed in from the outside to lever the handle up."

"Burglars!" said Moira. "Like we had before!"

"But that time they were after the TV and the electronic gear, till thanks to Tex and Sheelagh the Guards caught them just in time," Dick said. "Tonight, nothing's been taken."

"Except Fifi!" Patsy was sobbing again.

Tex looked at Sheelagh. They were both wondering whoever would want to steal a horrible cat like Fifi. And they were both thinking that if they had been in the house, they could have foiled the thieves like they did the last time.

"I'm afraid you're right, Patsy," said Dick. "It looks as if Fifi has been kidnapped."

Moira phoned the Guards and told them.

When she had finished she said: "They said they'd come round in the morning. Since nothing seems to have been stolen they suggested we lock up well now and tell them all about it tomorrow."

"But what about Fifi?" Patsy wailed.

"They said she had probably wandered off and would come back of her own accord. They couldn't spare anyone to go out in the middle of the night looking for a stray cat."

Dick and Moira made Patsy a cup of tea and tried their best to calm her down. When they had all gone to bed, Tex and Sheelagh talked. "This is a case for the Cat Watch Gang," said Tex. "Kidnapping is a serious crime."

"I suppose in this case we could call it CAT-NAPPING!" Sheelagh smiled. "But who would want to steal Fifi?"

"That's what we've got to find out. We know she's a pain in the neck, but there must be people who want her."

"Let's ask ourselves why they might want her, first of all," said Sheelagh. "That should give us some clues."

"A motive, that's what they call it," said Tex, remembering some of the detective programmes that Dick and Moira watched on the television. Tex couldn't really understand them, but people often talked about motives. It just meant the reason why someone would commit a crime.

"Well, what about revenge?" said Sheelagh.

"Revenge for what?"

"I know!" said Sheelagh. "It could be Paddy the window-cleaner. He hates us because we attacked him. Perhaps he decided to get his own back."

"But in that case surely, he would kidnap *us* and not Fifi. We're the ones who went after him."

"He knows we're too clever to be caught, so he took Fifi instead," said Sheelagh.

"Could be," said Tex. "Any other suspects?"

"What about Liam?"

"But again, it was *us* he didn't like, because we kept messing up his picture."

"Hey, but I've just remembered. He was talking to Dick about how hard it was to get work. That means he hasn't got much money."

"And we heard Julia Walsh say that Fifi must be worth a fortune!"

"That's it!" cried Sheelagh. "He kidnapped Fifi to sell her."

"We must stop him," said Tex. "However awful Fifi is, she doesn't deserve that."

"But how can we find her?" Sheelagh asked.

"If only we could tell Dick and Moira," said Tex. It was so irritating sometimes that people couldn't understand what cats were saying.

"Well, I suppose he won't be able to sell Fifi tonight. When the Guards come round tomorrow, maybe we can do something then."

The cat detectives talked on into the night. Just as Sheelagh was nodding off to sleep, her eyes glanced at a picture on the wall.

"Tex!" she called.

"What?" asked Tex sleepily from his armchair.

"That picture on the wall: Dick and Moira often look at it, and get all soppy. They say it's a picture of their wedding."

"Well, what about it?" asked Tex.

"I remember they once said that Liam took the picture!" said Sheelagh. "Supposing we knock it off the wall, they'll think of Liam, and maybe connect him with breaking into the house and taking Fifi."

"Maybe," said Tex doubtfully. "It's worth a try anyway."

"We'll do it tomorrow, when the Guards are here," said Sheelagh.

Next morning when the door-bell rang, Tex and Sheelagh climbed on to a chair near the picture, ready to jump up at it.

But when Dick opened the door, it wasn't the Guards. It was Liam himself.

"I just thought you'd like to have a look at these photos," he said. "I developed them last night. Fifi looks good in them. I'm sure Patsy will be pleased."

"He didn't mention the photographs of *us*," said Tex huffily.

"Come in, Liam – we've got some bad news," said Dick.

"Never mind that," said Sheelagh. "Let's hear what he says. He's got a nerve, coming round with pictures of Fifi when he's just kidnapped her."

Tex and Sheelagh sat under the dining-room table while Dick and Liam talked. Liam sounded upset when he heard that Fifi had disappeared. He even suggested that his pictures of Fifi could be used to help the Guards find the white Persian. They might put them in the paper.

"You see," said Sheelagh, "he'll even make some money from that."

237

When the Guards came, they looked at the pictures, and said they would take one for their files. They examined the window in Patsy's room and agreed it looked as if someone had forced it open. But they said the cat probably jumped out then, and ran off somewhere. They were sure it would make its own way back.

Tex and Sheelagh were not so sure.

"When Liam leaves," said Tex, "we'll follow him home, and find Fifi." They went out to discuss it with the rest of the Cat Watch Gang in the lane.

"Why should he help the Guards if he's the thief?" asked Butterscotch.

"To put them off the scent," said Tex.

"Talking of scent," said Guinness, "maybe we should send Wolf on the trail of Fifi. He could track her down!"

"And we could all follow," said Sheelagh.

"We might have to go for miles and miles," said Butterscotch, who was so lazy she thought it was a long journey if she had to move from her bed to her bowl of food.

"But we've got to try," said Wolf. "I'll do my best, anyway."

"Well, you get the prize for tracking, Wolf," said Guinness.

"The prize!" said Sheelagh. "That's another motive!"

"What do you mean?" asked Tex.

"The prize in the Cat Show, for Persian Longhairs. Julia Walsh said Fifi might win it. But who else wants to win it?"

"Well, who?" Butterscotch was bewildered.

"Julia Walsh herself!" said Sheelagh. "With that champion cat she was boasting about. She's the one who would really like Fifi to disappear! She could be the kidnapper!"

"So that's three suspects!" said Tex. "Paddy, Liam, and Julia Walsh."

"Which one shall we go after first?" asked Guinness.

"We've no time to lose," said Sheelagh. "We'll go after them all, at the same time."

# 8

## On the Trail

"Here's my plan," said Sheelagh. "We split into three teams, each going after one of the suspects. Then we meet back here in two hours' time, and give our reports."

They decided that Sheelagh should team up with Guinness, and Tex with Butterscotch.

"That makes us the Black-and-White Team, and the Ginger Team," said Tex.

"But that leaves Wolf to be a team on his own," said Guinness.

"Just tell me what to do, and I'll do it," said Wolf, wagging his tail enthusiastically.

"You're the best tracker," said Sheelagh. "Now we know Paddy's been up and down this lane, so if you can find his scent, you can trail him to where he lives, and see if he's got Fifi."

Wolf began sniffing around on the ground. Soon he said: "I've got it. See you later!"

The dog went away down the lane, his nose to the ground.

"Butterscotch and I will wait by the front gate," said Tex. "Then, when Liam leaves, we'll follow him."

"What about Julia Walsh?" asked Guinness. "We don't know where she lives."

"We know Dick passes her Cattery when he goes jogging," Sheelagh said. "He should be going out soon, like he does every morning. We'll follow him."

"Let's go, Butterscotch!" cried Tex. Reluctantly, the lazy cat got up and followed him. Sheelagh and Guinness sat down to wait for Dick to set off on his jogging trip.

Wolf reached the end of the lane, and stopped. Cars were going past, and people walked by him on the footpath. He wasn't supposed to be out on his own. He was usually taken for walks on a lead, then let out to run in the park or in the woods.

He knew he must stay on the footpath, or the

cars would mow him down. He put his nose to the ground again. Yes, Paddy's scent was still there, but Wolf felt there was another scent mixed in with it – the scent of a dog.

He followed both scents down the street, till the trail turned off down another street. Then Paddy's scent seemed to disappear. Wolf thought he must have got into a car at this point.

What could he do now? He sniffed around along the footpath for a while. He was in luck. The scent of the dog appeared again.

Wolf followed the trail down several roads until he came to a row of houses with gates and small gardens. He moved along, looking in at each gate. At the fifth gate, he found himself staring into a long-nosed, long-eared face on the other side.

"Hello, hello, hello!" barked the other face.

Wolf barked a hello in return. He had met the dog he'd been trailing. It was a spaniel, with floppy ears and a slobbery mouth, and it was wagging its little tail so hard that Wolf thought it would shake its whole rear end off.

They introduced themselves. The spaniel's name was Roddy.

He was very talkative, and before long he had told Wolf all about the people in his house, who were called Paddy and Molly, and had three children.

"What does Paddy do?" asked Wolf.

"He goes out every day with a ladder," said Roddy. "He cleans people's windows."

Wolf knew he had come to the right place. "I am a detective," he said. "We are looking for a lost cat."

"Why?" asked Roddy. "The more cats that get lost, the better, that's what I say."

"Some of them are quite pleasant, really," said Wolf, defending his friends.

"They're no friends of mine," growled Roddy. "If I see one anywhere near me, I frighten it away in double-quick time." He rushed around the garden giving furious barks and snarls, to show how he dealt with cats.

"Then, Paddy didn't bring a cat back to the house here last night at all? A long-haired white cat?"

"You must be joking! I wouldn't have let it in the door. Besides, cats make Molly sneeze. She won't have them in the house."

Wolf said goodbye to Roddy, who told him to come and say hello again some time.

"Thanks, I will," said Wolf. Then he remembered some words he had heard at home when Mr Rooney was reading crime stories aloud from the paper.

Wolf nodded to Roddy and said: "Thank you for helping us with our inquiries."

Tex and Butterscotch were hiding behind a bush near the front gate of Dick and Moira's house. Liam came out with his spotlight and his case of camera equipment. He put them on the back seat of a small red car. He left the door open as he turned to go back up the path and say goodbye to Dick.

"Come on!" said Tex. The cats ran through the gate and jumped into the car. They crouched down under the front seats. Liam didn't notice them at all, when he got in the car and drove away.

He drove to a place where the streets were very busy and Tex and Butterscotch could hear the roar of traffic and the hooting of car horns. Liam turned down a quieter side street and parked the car. He twisted round and reached out towards the back seat. Tex and Butterscotch were afraid he'd see them, but he just took a small black object out of the case, and turned to the front again.

They heard some beeps as Liam dialled a number on his mobile phone. Tex realised what it was – he had seen Dick and Moira using one.

They listened. "Hello, is that the Daily Journal?" said Liam. "Can I speak to Harry Galvin, the Pictures Editor?" There was a pause, then he went on: "Harry? Hi, it's Liam. Listen, you know those pictures I was taking for you, about the cats in the Cat Show? Well, something's happened, and I have a picture you may want to use in the news pages."

He explained all about Fifi and her disappearance. Then Harry must have asked if there was a reward, because Liam said:

"There may be a reward, but I'm not bothered about that. You can say the paper will give it to a cat charity, if you like. But I would like to find that cat. It seemed very pleased with itself, but I think underneath it's probably quite timid. I'm sure it must be very frightened. I'd hate anything to happen to it."

There was another pause while Harry said something. Then Liam said: "That's fine. I'm only a few streets away from your office, I'll bring the pictures in straight away."

When Liam reached the office and got out of the car, Tex said: "It doesn't sound as if Liam could have taken Fifi. He doesn't want a reward, and he seemed really keen to find her."

There was no reply. "Butterscotch?" said Tex. Then he heard gentle snoring coming from under the seat beside him.

"Wake up!" he said. They talked about what

Liam had said, and decided to report that he wasn't a likely suspect after all.

"There's just one problem," said Butterscotch. "We've no idea where we are. How can we report anything, if we can't get home?"

# 9

## Meeting the Duchess

Tex was worried. If they stayed in the car and got out at Liam's house, they would still have no idea where they were. And they couldn't hide in the car for ever.

"I know!" said Tex. "When he comes back, we'll show ourselves."

"He might just turn us out," said Butterscotch.

"It's our only chance," said Tex.

So when Liam got back into the car, Tex and Butterscotch scrambled out from their hiding-place and got on to the front seat beside him.

"Hello there!" said Tex.

"Here we are!" said Butterscotch.

Liam was astonished to see two cats suddenly

appear from nowhere and make loud miaows at him. Then he recognised Tex.

"Stowaways!" he laughed. "Well, what are we going to do with you?"

Tex looked at him appealingly, his eyes wide.

"I guess I'd better take you home," said Liam. "Otherwise Dick and Moira will think *you've* been kidnapped as well as Fifi."

Sheelagh and Guinness waited quite a while in the lane. Then Guinness said gloomily: "Suppose he decides not to go jogging today?"

Sheelagh had thought of that too, but she was determined to be cheerful. "We'll just have to think of another way of finding the Cattery."

She had absolutely no idea what way that might be, so she was relieved when she saw Dick come out into the garden in his jogging track-suit. He opened the gate and ran off down the lane. Sheelagh and Guinness followed, keeping at a distance so that he wouldn't notice them.

Dick jogged into the street at the end of the lane, then along the footpath of the busy road. One or two passers-by looked curiously at the two cats trotting purposefully along. A small girl tried to pick Sheelagh up, but she wriggled free and went on her way.

Dick turned down a quiet road that led off the main road. At the end of it was a gate leading into a small park. Dick jogged across it on the grass. Suddenly Sheelagh saw a small, yapping dog running towards them. It reached them, hoping they'd run away in fear, so that he could chase them. So he was very surprised when the two cats stood their ground and bared their fangs at him.

Sheelagh shouted: "Get lost, fish-face!"

Guinness snarled: "Yeah, you heard her – get lost!"

They both took a step forward with a paw in the air, ready to hit out at the dog. Just then they heard the rasping voice of a woman across the park, calling: "Bingo, come here! Come here at once!"

"Sorry, I've got to go," said the dog thankfully. He turned and ran away as fast as his small legs would carry him.

Dick came to a gate at the other side of the park. There was a road, and on the far side of it a gateway with some trees, and a drive leading to a big stone house. There was a gate with a stone pillar on either side, and each pillar had a statue of a cat on top of it. There was a sign too, with big letters.

They saw Dick stop at the gate, wondering whether to go in.

"I'm sure this is the place," said Sheelagh. They saw Dick go up the drive and knock at the green front door. Sheelagh and Guinness jumped up and each hid themselves behind one of the stone cats on top of the pillars.

Mrs Walsh opened the door, and she and Dick had a conversation. The cats were too far away to hear much, but they did catch the words, "Oh, I'm so sorry," from Mrs Walsh.

Then as Dick turned to go, they heard her say, "Please let me know if there's anything I can do."

Sheelagh and Guinness watched Dick jog back through the gate below them, and go on up the road.

"Right," said Sheelagh. "Let's take a look."

They went round the side of the house. At the back there was a large garden with a lawn and bushes and trees, and beyond it a fenced off area, with a long, low wooden building behind it. The fenced area had wire netting all around and above it. Sheelagh could see two or three cats peering through the wire.

"That must be the Cattery," said Sheelagh.

Then they heard a voice quite near them saying: "Hello!" The voice came from a glassed-in conservatory at the back of the house. There was an open window in it with a wire screen, and behind the screen was sitting a large fluffy white cat, staring at them with orange eyes.

"It's Fifi!" cried Guinness, and they both bounded across the grass to the window.

"Fifi, we've come to rescue you!" said Sheelagh.

The cat stared at them, puzzled. "What are you on about?" he asked.

"Aren't you Fifi?" asked Guinness.

"Certainly not!" said the cat haughtily. "I am the Duchess of Dingle. And I don't know who you are, but you'd better get back into your own quarters, quick sharp. You're not supposed to be out."

"We're not boarding cats," said Sheelagh. "We're cat detectives. We're looking for a cat like you who's been kidnapped."

"There *is* no cat like me," said the Duchess. "I wish there were, sometimes. It's lonely being a champion – and boring too, with only Julia for company. And she's always going on at me to stand up straight, and stop yawning."

The cats told the Duchess about Fifi, and asked if she had seen anything suspicious.

"Come to think of it," said the Duchess. "When I was sleeping over there on my cushion last night, I did think I heard a cat's voice, and then Julia saying: 'Sssssh!' I just thought it was one of the cats who'd got out of the Cattery."

"It sounds as if we're on the right track," said Sheelagh.

She and Guinness crept through the bushes in the garden till they came to the fence with the wire netting. They looked through. Now they could see that the open area inside was wired off into separate pens, and each of them had an opening at the end leading into the wooden building. That must be where each cat had its sleeping quarters.

They moved along the fence, talking to any cats that were near it. None of them had heard anything unusual in the night. There were always a few cats out whingeing at the moon, and saying they wanted to go home.

"One of them could have been Fifi!" said Sheelagh.

They moved along to the end of the fence, and round the side.

They noticed that the door at the end of

the last pen wasn't open like the rest, but shut up.

They went along the side of the fence. Suddenly Sheelagh said: "Listen!"

From behind the closed door they could just hear a faint and familiar voice crying: "Help! Help!"

Guinness and Sheelagh looked at each other.

"Fifi, is that you?" called Sheelagh.

"It is!" said Fifi. "Oh, Sheelagh, I'm so glad to hear you!"

"Keep calm," said Sheelagh. "We'll get you out of there."

"Wonderful! But how?"

"We'll come back tonight, when it's dark, with reinforcements!"

Just then they saw Julia Walsh coming across the lawn from the house. She was carrying a bowl. She went round the far side of the wooden building, then they saw her enter a door at the back. It must lead to the sleeping quarters behind the pens.

Sheelagh and Guinness stayed listening. Now, through the door they could hear Julia Walsh's voice talking to Fifi.

"There you are, Fifi, there's some lovely food for you. There's a good cat. Don't worry, you won't come to any harm. I'd just like you to stay here till after the Cat Show, that's all."

Sheelagh turned to Guinness and whispered: "We'll make sure Fifi is out of there a lot sooner than that!"

# 10

## The Great Escape

Sheelagh and Guinness ran round the Cattery and back across the lawn towards the house. The Duchess of Dingle was watching them through the wire screen. Sheelagh waved, and was about to stop and talk when they saw Julia Walsh come out of the Cattery at the far side of the garden.

"We must get out of here," said Guinness. They dashed round to the front of the house, and out of the gate.

When they got back into the lane, the others were waiting for them. Wolf told how he had talked to Paddy's dog, and Tex and Butterscotch described their car journey with Liam.

"Two suspects eliminated," said Tex. "Which means Julia Walsh must be the kidnapper."

"And she *is*!" cried Sheelagh. She and Guinness told the story of their journey, and their discovery of where Fifi was hidden.

"A pity we can't tell Patsy," said Butterscotch.

"We could try, but she wouldn't understand a word," said Guinness.

"Well," said Sheelagh impatiently, "if people won't learn our language, what can we do about it?"

The Cat Watch Gang gathered in a circle, to plan that night's OPERATION RESCUE.

Dick and Moira and Patsy were out for much of the day, asking neighbours if they had seen anything of Fifi, and pinning LOST notices and descriptions of her on lamp-posts.

Tex and Sheelagh slept a lot of the time, so they would have energy for the night's expedition.

As soon as it started to get dark, the CAT WATCH GANG gathered in the lane.

"All ready?" said Tex. Everyone nodded.

"Right," said Sheelagh, "let's launch OPERATION RESCUE!"

She and Guinness led the way down the lane and out into the road, then along the footpaths that led to the park. If people had looked curiously at two cats padding along this morning, the sight of four cats and a dog following each other in single file really made them stare and point and chuckle.

The Gang were glad to get into the park. They made their way across it as the night grew dark. There was a wind getting up, and heavy clouds in the sky.

As they reached Julia Walsh's house, they felt a few spots of rain. They crept round the side of the house.

"We must sneak past the conservatory, lying very flat, in case someone's in there who might see us," said Sheelagh.

The conservatory was lit up inside, but no one was there except the Duchess of Dingle lying on her cushion. She was fast asleep.

They crept across the lawn, feeling the patter of rain on their backs. They went round the side of the Cattery and found the door at the back.

Guinness stood on his hind legs and pulled down the handle, and the others pushed the door open. They went into a long, dimly-lit corridor, with a line of small closed doors on one side, which must lead into the pens and the living quarters.

The Gang filed along past the closed doors to the end of the line, where they knew Fifi was being kept. From behind the doors they heard cats disturbed from sleep saying: "Who's that?" and "What's going on?"

But they kept on until they reached the final door. Tex tapped on it with his paw and whispered: "Fifi! We're here!"

There was no reply. "She must be asleep," said Sheelagh, and gave another tap. Still no reply.

"Perhaps Mrs Walsh has moved her," said Guinness, always ready to see the gloomy side of things.

"I'll see if *I* can wake her," said Wolf. He gave a low growl.

There was a chorus of alarm from the cats in the other pens when they heard Wolf:

"I heard a dog!"

"Get that beast away!"

"Beware of the Dog!"

"Take cover!"

"Shut up!" yelled Tex, afraid that the row would be heard outside. Then he called out: "It's not a real dog. I was just doing an imitation." Then he whispered to Wolf: "Sorry about that."

The cats' shouts subsided into mutterings about bad jokes and disturbing a night's sleep.

Then from behind Fifi's door they heard the Persian's voice:

"Tex and Sheelagh – I'm here! I knew you'd come."

"Hold on," said Sheelagh. "We'll soon have the door open." But it wasn't as easy as that. The door was locked firmly shut. No amount of pushing and scratching would move it. Wolf tried taking a run and hurling himself at it, but even that didn't work.

"I know," said Sheelagh, "we'll go outside again, and make a hole in the wire netting."

The Gang trooped out of the building and round to the front. They all gnawed at parts of the wire in a circle, so that they were weakened.

261

Then Wolf grabbed the middle of the circle in his jaws, and pulled and pulled. The cats tried to help by holding his paws and pulling backwards when he did. Finally the wire snapped and Wolf and the rest of them fell backwards in a heap.

Sheelagh and Tex dashed through the hole and ran to the door at the far end of the pen. Luckily this one had a simple bolt which the kittens were easily able to slide open.

Fifi came out and followed them back across the pen. The hole in the wire netting was just wide enough for Fifi to squeeze through, though she left a few strands of fur on the spikes of wire

"Thank you, thank you!" she said. "You're wonderful!" She began giving a licking kiss to all the cats in turn, and to Wolf too.

"Thanks, Fifi," said Sheelagh. "It's all in a day's work, for the CAT WATCH GANG!"

The rain was falling steadily as they made their way silently back across the lawn towards the house. They could see the Duchess of Dingle still asleep on her cushion. They were just creeping past the conservatory windows when they heard the voice of Julia Walsh, inside.

"Here's your dinner, Duchess!" she said.

Sheelagh said: "Freeze!" and they all crouched down, totally still. They could see Julia Walsh put a fancy silver bowl of food down on the floor, as she stroked the Duchess of Dingle. The Duchess yawned, jumped down from her cushion, and began munching at the bowl.

"There you are!" said Julia Walsh. "A nice dinner and a good night's sleep, and you'll run away with the first prize tomorrow. There'll be no competition from your rival, Fifi – because she won't even be there!"

Outside, Wolf was feeling very wet as the rain came down. He longed to shake himself to get rid of the water, like he did when he came out of the sea, making all the family leap out of the way so as not to get wet. He stood there shivering. Then, worst of all, he felt a sneeze coming on. He just couldn't contain it, and finally a loud "AAAH-CHOO!" sounded in the night.

Julia Walsh looked up, startled. "What was that?" she said.

The Duchess looked up too. They both moved in the direction of the window where the CAT WATCH GANG were crouching outside.

"Is anyone there?" said Julia, peering through the glass. Because of the dark and the rain, she couldn't see much with the lights of the conservatory on. But the Duchess of Dingle had come to the wire screen and was gazing out. In the dark, she could see better than Julia. And she found herself staring straight into Sheelagh's eyes.

"Hello again," said the Duchess.

"What are you miaowing for?" said Julia. "Can you see someone out there?"

Sheelagh leaned forward and whispered: "Don't give us away, Duchess. Cats must stick together!"

The Duchess smiled. Sheelagh wondered what she would do.

Would she give them away, and make sure Fifi was caught again?

But then the Duchess said: "Come back and see me some time, will you? If you can get that Fifi out, I'm sure you can find a way to get me out too. Then we could chat and play together."

"It's a deal," said Sheelagh.

Julia was still peering through the window, worried that all this miaowing from the Duchess must mean someone was outside. She was just about to open a window, when suddenly the Duchess raced to the other side of the conservatory, then rushed back to her cushion and grabbed it in her jaws and began shaking it. Julia Walsh ran after her, crying: "Duchess, Duchess! What's the matter?"

She reached out to stroke the cat, but the Persian dropped the cushion and ran out of the conservatory through the door that led into the house.

"Come back, come back!" said Julia, following her.

The CAT WATCH GANG breathed a sigh of relief.

"Good for the Duchess!" said Tex. "She distracted Julia so that we could get away."

"Let's go!" said Sheelagh. They all dashed round to the front of the house, along the drive and out of the gate, yelping and cheering with delight as they splashed their way home through the rain.

There was a great reunion that night between Patsy and Fifi. She and Dick and Moira wondered where Fifi, and indeed Tex and Sheelagh, had been: they were so wet and muddy from their night journey.

Fifi thanked Tex and Sheelagh for their brilliant OPERATION RESCUE. She said she was sorry if she'd been stuck-up and rude to them. She was so used to being told that she was special, and that all that mattered was looking well-groomed and highly bred, so as to win a Cat Show Prize.

Now she realised that making friends and having fun were much more important. She said shyly: "And tomorrow, if you don't mind, I'd love to take part in some of your Olympic Games practices."

"Delighted!" said Sheelagh and Tex together.

The next day, Fifi was out in the lane bright and early with the rest of them. The rain had stopped but the ground was still muddy and wet. Nobody minded. They did fence-walking, and high jumps and long jumps, and tail-chasing, and wrestling, and rolling-over-and-over.

By the time Dick and Moira shouted out of the back door that their breakfast was ready, they were covered in mud. Fifi's white fur was all streaked and matted and dirty, and the fur on her head stuck up like a crazy wig, with her two orange eyes gleaming in her mucky face.

Patsy shrieked when she looked out of the courtyard gate.

"Fifi! What have you been doing? Oh, I'll never get her cleaned up in time for the Cat Show now!"

"Never mind," said Moira, "she seems to be

enjoying herself more than she would at a Cat Show."

"Oh, I am! I am!" said Fifi, turning a somersault. "Thanks to Tex and Sheelagh!"

"You're welcome, Fifi," said Sheelagh, and all three of them jumped on to the fence and did a celebration fence-walk.

Wolf and Butterscotch and Guinness cheered. And so did Dick and Moira, and Patsy.

# THE MYSTERY OF MONK ISLAND

by

## GORDON SNELL

A week's boating holiday on a lake is an exciting prospect for Brendan, his friend Dessy and his cousin Molly. But Emer, daughter of the high-powered businessman who has hired the boat, seems determined to mess things up for everyone.

There are much bigger problems, though, when someone disappears and ruthless kidnappers demand a ransom.

Left alone on the boat, the young people have to cope by themselves. Should they go to the authorities, or would that mean they would never see the victim alive again? Who are the ghostly figures that lurk on Monk Island at night? The island is full of dangers: there are traps and snares, creatures in the woods and weird chanting sounds among the ruins. Meanwhile, the kidnappers are beginning to lose patience . . .

ISBN 1-85371-551-4

# DANGEROUS TREASURE

by

## GORDON SNELL

Brendan plans a summer holiday of wild adventures with his friend Dessy in Dublin and then finds he has to stay with his cousin Molly in the country.

The visit, however, turns out to be full of excitement and menace, as an ancient Celtic brooch from a nearby haunted castle is stolen, and the three young people become the target of a criminal gang.

There are horseback chases, kidnappings, and eerie happenings among the castle ruins as the ghost of a murdered princess seems about to take her dreadful revenge . . .

ISBN 1-85371-420-8